I0534976

FAITHVILLE

A COMMUNITY CHANGED

JAMES K. RUSHING

FAITHVILLE

Copyright © 2024 by James K. Rushing.

All rights reserved. No part of this publication may be reproduced, distributed, or transmitted in any form or by any means, including photocopying, recording, or other electronic or mechanical methods, without the written consent of the publisher. The only exceptions are for brief quotations included in critical reviews and other noncommercial uses permitted by copyright law.

MILTON & HUGO L.L.C.

4407 Park Ave., Suite 5

Union City, NJ 07087, USA

Website: *www. miltonandhugo.com*

Hotline: *1- 888-778-0033*

Email: *info@miltonandhugo.com*

Ordering Information:

Quantity sales. Special discounts are granted to corporations, associations, and other organizations. For more information on these discounts, please reach out to the publisher using the contact information provided above.

Library of Congress Control Number:		2024907829
ISBN-13:	979-8-89285-060-5	[Paperback Edition]
	979-8-89285-061-2	[Hardback Edition]
	979-8-89285-059-9	[Digital Edition]

Rev. date: 04/17/2024

Dedication

"To Leslie.
My partner, my best friend, my muse, my greatest supporter, my love."

Contents

Acknowledgments

Any good that may come from this book comes directly from God. For many years, I have wanted to write my thoughts about worship but never had the time, desire, or energy. The Holy Spirit started moving heavily in my life the last quarter of 2023. It was by this movement that the book was completed.

This book would never have happened if not for the wonderful encouragement from my best friend and life partner, Leslie W. Tombleson Rewald. Our continual discussions about God, church, worship, theology, psychology, and various other subjects all pointed toward the need for a book like this. She listened, she read, she made comments, and talked me through multiple scenarios to help get it finished. She was there all the way.

David and Linda Croxton spent hours upon hours editing my drafts and calling attention to the minor details that needed attention. Without their edits and encouragement, this book probably still wouldn't be finished.

Sharon Cox read my completed draft and made comments that supported the fact that this book was indeed written for a purpose. She shared that she had experienced many incidents written in these pages.

Chapter

ONE

THE PLACE

Just off Highway 84 in South Central Georgia lies a quiet little town called Faithville. The population was 4,265 at the last census. Most people here are middle class, and of course, there are the wealthy and the poor. The city is busy with the usual gas stations, shopping centers, coffee shops, antique stores, clothes stores, sports stores, etc. It's racially diverse—with whites, blacks, Hispanics, and Asians. Over half the people were born and raised here, and their families before them have been here for generations. Everyone seems to know everyone else, and they all appear to get along quite well. Because of this, the crime rate is low—typically, all are related to teenagers getting into harmless mischief.

Though there are many places to eat in Faithville, Dauphy's Diner is the hot spot for hungry people and the best place to hear what's going on in the town. Of course, for more intimate chatter (or gossip), you could visit Millie's Boutique or Fred's Barber Shop to hear what may or may not be true.

The police station houses a chief, an investigator, and one police officer. It's small, but then there is very little crime, so there's no need to increase the size.

It's fall in Faithville, and the temperatures have dropped from the overly hot summer to a nice mid-fifties in the evenings and upper sixties during the day. It's harvest season for the cotton crop. The cotton crop and the gin make up the main industry in Faithville and a large number of the people are employed in the cotton industry.

The town has an abundance of small churches averaging from 25 to 30 members up to 150 or so. In the city proper are the mainline denominations, and on the outskirts are the independent churches and the churches not affiliated with any denomination.

And that's where the story begins. On any given Sunday, most churches have less than a quarter of their sanctuary filled with people. It has been this way for years. People just seemed to have lost sight of the importance of worshiping on Sunday morning. Some churches have more, some have less; but overall, going to church has lost its appeal.

Holy Cross Church has been at the center of Faithville's history for over 125 years. Its classic cruciform style, stained glass windows, and the only real pipe organ in town make it a favored stop of visitors and passersby. Father Greene has been the rector there for the last twenty-three years. Even though the church is the centerpiece of the town, they have their issues with church attendance as well.

Chapter

TWO

THE SUGGESTION

Holy Cross Church

Father Greene ended the church service with a benediction. "Now may the grace of God, the love of Jesus, and the sweet communion of the Holy Spirit, rest, rule, and abide now, henceforth, and forevermore. Amen."

Outside, Father Greene shook hands with parishioners as they were leaving. A middle-aged man and his wife shook hands with Father Greene and introduced themselves as Ted and Alicia Wilson.

Father Greene said, "I'm pleased to meet you and so glad you chose to worship with us today."

Ted asked if there might be some time this week that they could speak. They arranged a day and time for the meeting and said their goodbyes.

Later that week, Father Greene, Ted, and Alicia met in his office. Mrs. Alexander, the parish secretary, brought in a tray of coffee and blueberry scones.

After some coffee, scones, and the exchange of some pleasantries, Father Greene asked, "So, what can I do for you?"

Ted said, "It's not really what you can do for us but what we can do for you."

"Oh," said Father Greene. "What can you do for me?"

Ted and Alicia looked at each other and smiled.

Alicia said, "We can help you grow your church!"

"Marvelous," said Father Greene. "What did you have in mind?"

Ted and Alicia started chattering about all the changes that would need to be made to the sanctuary, mission statement, worship practices, music, and the like.

Father Greene couldn't get a word in, though he tried. After they had wound down a bit, he interrupted and suggested that all the ideas be written down so they could be submitted for review to the church leadership.

Ted had a bit of a frown on his face and said to Father Greene. "I thought you were in charge here!"

Father Greene said, "I am the spiritual leader of this parish, which means I oversee spiritual matters, but the church leaders all guide the church forward."

Ted said, "Well, I guess we need to be talking to someone else."

He and Alicia stood, shook Father Greene's hand, thanked him for his time, and left.

Father Greene looked a bit perplexed and just sat there and thought for a little while.

A few days later, one of the church leaders called the church office and asked for Father Greene.

Mrs. Alexander said, "Father Greene, Larry Pritchard is on the phone for you."

Father Greene picked up the phone and said, "Hello, Larry. How are you?"

They chatted for a few minutes before Larry said, "Ted Wilson came to visit me at my house and brought a list of changes that the church should make if we ever intend to grow. And he said it was your idea."

Father Greene stopped Larry from continuing and said, "Wait a minute, Larry. Let's get things straight before you continue. Ted and Alicia wanted to meet with me, and we met yesterday in my office. They were going on about how they were going to help us grow the church and started spurting out all these ideas. I simply told them they would need to make a list to be submitted to the church leadership."

Larry said, "Oh. That makes sense."

Father Greene added, "I think it somewhat improper for Ted to start visiting church leaders to push an agenda."

Larry said, "I agree. He has also visited at least a couple more of the leadership. I know this because they have already called me. I believe it's time we had a meeting with the church leaders."

A meeting was called for on Thursday evening. All the church leaders showed up, and they were all carrying a file folder, presumably with the list that Ted had compiled.

Father Greene called the meeting to order and began with a prayer. After the prayer, he continued, "Now, we are here because a parishioner came to me earlier this week and suggested that he was going to help us grow the church. When he found that I was not the final decision maker, he took it upon himself to come to all of you. I suggested he make a list to be submitted to all of you, but I never thought he would come to you individually."

Sammy Samuels spoke up. "That's not how we do things. We have a meeting and decide together, right?"

Everyone agreed. "Yes, that is right!"

Father Greene warned them that this could turn bad very quickly if they were not all on the same page. "I am here as your rector to provide spiritual guidance. You, my friends, are the decision-making body of the church. So with that behind us, let's look at the list. Does anyone have an extra copy? I don't seem to have received one."

Edward Reece said, "Father Greene, you didn't get a list?"

Father Greene said, "No, I didn't."

Edward looked puzzled.

A copy was made for Father Greene, and they all started reading down the list. The first item on the list was to change the colors of the church. Well, the church was old and could use a good paint job inside and out, but the budget wasn't healthy enough to allow it without a fundraiser. Everyone agreed that was a good idea and would probably attract more people.

The next item was that the carpet needed to be replaced with either a painted cement floor or maybe hardwood flooring. Again, that would be nice, but the budget funds were too low. Everyone agreed.

Sammy said, "It looks like if we want to grow, we must shell out some money."

Other comments were made, like, "Yeah, everything costs, and we already give until it hurts."

As the perusal of the list continued, it became apparent that very little could be accomplished so far without putting the church into debt, which wasn't something that anyone wanted.

Pete Elliot, who had been quiet for most of the meeting, spoke up. "Fr. Greene, I've looked a little farther down the list, and there are some entries here that I think cause us some questions. For instance, on page 3, Ted suggests we cut some prayers, shorten the sermons, and add some electric guitars."

Father Greene said, "Oh my!"

Pete continued, "I believe these items fall under the spiritual guidance of our rector."

Everyone agreed!

"Well," said Father Greene, "may I suggest that we table these suggestions until we have all had time to think about what items are doable and how much fundraising would be involved."

All agreed, and the meeting was adjourned.

Father Greene began to feel uneasy about all that had happened the past couple of days and found it difficult to sleep. He rose early the next morning and began his daily office, which he had done faithfully for the past forty years. The scripture readings seemed to all be related to "being faithful." He knew that God speaks in mysterious ways and pondered what the scriptures were speaking of and what God might be telling him.

As he sipped his morning coffee, he remembered the story of Daniel and how he was faithful to God. Also, the Hebrew children were faithful to God and would not bow to an idol to save themselves from the fiery furnace. He had to be on guard, and he had to be vigilant to protect his flock from any deception. He thought it may be a good idea to find out more about the Wilsons.

Father Greene showed up at the police station and asked to speak with his friend the police chief.

"Good morning, Father Greene," said Chief Peters.

"And a good morning to you, Chief Peters," said Father Greene. "I'm wondering if I might have a word with you privately."

"Of course," said the chief. "Let's go to my office."

After some chitchat about the family and the weather, the chief looked at Father Greene and said, "What did you want to talk about?"

Father Greene explained what had happened at the church after meeting the Wilsons. He continued that he was a bit troubled about what might be going on and asked if the chief could shed any light on the Wilsons.

"Are they new in town? Just passing through? Anything?" asked Father Greene.

Chief Peters said that he met them at Dauphy's Diner a few days ago but didn't know much about them. "I'll see what I can find out about them, and if there's anything to be concerned about, I'll let you know."

Father Greene was pleased. "Thank you so much, Chief Peters."

Regular church council meetings were held every month on the first Wednesday of the month at 6:00 p.m. That night had come, and all the council members were present.

The senior warden, Eric Dooley, called the meeting to order, and Father Greene led them in a short devotional from the scriptures he had read that morning. After that, he led them in a short prayer asking God to help them to always be faithful to the One we worship.

Then Eric reminded them that the last time they met, they were discussing a list that was presented to them by Ted Wilson. It had been tabled until everyone had the chance to read through the list and discern what should be given attention to and what should be ignored.

"Does anyone want to start us off with their thoughts?" asked Eric.

Sammy Samuels said, "I've been considering what the list is suggesting about updates to the sanctuary with paint and flooring. Considering the size of the church, I estimate that would cost somewhere in the neighborhood of $20,000."

Edward Reese said, "Whew! That's a lot of money for just paint and flooring."

"I know," said Sammy. "That includes the labor."

Pete Elliot said, "How much would we save if we did some or all of the work ourselves?"

Sammy said, "Probably about half that if there are people in our church that know how to put down flooring or paint."

"Even ten thousand dollars is a lot of money for us to raise," said Edward.

Eric said, "This is a time when I think we must dream a little and weigh the finances against the possibilities. Will more people come? And is that our goal?"

"If we want more people to come, then we must do something," said Sammy.

Then Pete said, "I guess the real question is, do we want more people to come? Father Greene, is that the right question?"

Father Greene said, "Pete, I think you're right. Church growth has been a hot topic in religious circles for the past decade. It seems that is the measuring stick for churches. They suggest that if you are not growing, then you're dying. My question would be, does 'growth' refer to numbers, faith, disciples, stewardship, or what?"

Everyone stopped and pondered the question.

"It's a hard question, Father Greene," said Eric, "but it's one we need to discern. If we are interested in just numbers, we could use that money to give out free pizza. Then the whole town would come.

But if we want to grow the church with servants for the Lord, we might want to look at this a bit differently."

Leon Wilkerson spoke up. "I've been noticing that our parish is getting older. We don't have many young people at all. If things keep going the way they are, in another fifteen to twenty years, there won't be any people left. The average age of our church is about seventy-two."

"That's a good point," said Sammy.

"Yes, it is," echoed a few others.

"Okay," said Father Greene. "Maybe we should back up and ask ourselves why people go to church, any church, on a given Lord's Day?"

The answers were all over the chart. Some said the sermon, some said the singing, some said activities, some said fellowship, and one person even said duty. It was now 7:25 p.m., and not one item had been decided on.

"Is there a reason that we have to decide on any of these items tonight?" asked Father Greene. "I think the hour is late, and we should adjourn for the night, promising that we will all ponder why people go to church and compare it with why they 'should' go to church."

Everyone agreed, and they adjourned with a prayer, asking God to guide them in their thoughts about faithfulness and discernment.

Freedom Church

Across town was a newer church, fifteen years old. It was a metal structure that looked a lot like a gymnasium or a multipurpose building. The pastor was Rick Marshall, a well-known and highly respected man in Faithville. Inside the church was plush carpet, sound absorbers on the textured walls, theatrical lighting, and a decent sound system that was controlled from a booth centered in the back of the room.

Pastor Marshall had just finished counseling a couple that was soon to be married when his secretary, Penny, buzzed his phone and said, "Pastor, there's a couple here to see you if you have time."

Pastor Marshall said, "Please show them in."

Penny opened the door and introduced the couple. "Pastor Marshall, these are Ted and Alicia Wilson."

They greeted each other with handshakes and sat down.

Pastor Marshall said, "Well, Ted and Alicia, what can I do for you?"

Again, Ted and Alicia looked at each other and smiled. Alicia said, "It's not what you can do for us but what we can do for you."

Pastor Marshall said, "Oh. What might that be?"

Ted and Alicia said in unison, "We are going to help you grow your church!"

"Wonderful!" exclaimed Pastor Marshall. "How will you do that?"

And just like with Father Greene, Ted and Alicia started chattering about all the changes that would need to be made.

Pastor Marshall couldn't interrupt, nor did he want to. He was hearing excitement and enthusiasm from these two strangers. He let them talk until they had run out of things to say.

Pastor Marshall said, "Do you have all these things written down?"

Ted said, "Why? Are you not the decision maker for this church?"

"Yes, I am," said Pastor Marshall. "I just want to see what all you are talking about doing before I can make any kind of decision on what we can and can't do."

From Ted's briefcase, he presented a list to Pastor Marshall. As the pastor perused the list, he noticed the suggestion for changes to the service. He asked, "Have you been to our services recently?"

"Yes," they both replied. "We were here about a month ago and evaluated everything."

"Well, this is quite a list," said Pastor Marshall. "And all in one visit? Is this something you have done before?"

Ted said, "Well, I've studied 'growth' for the past ten years, and I think I have a handle on what works, especially in churches, and what doesn't work. For instance, people go to church to be enlightened, entertained, and enthused. We call it the 3 E's."

"Well, that's a pretty impressive list you have, Ted. Have you seen church growth happen with these changes in other churches?"

Ted didn't hesitate to say, "Yes, all over the place."

"Can you give me an example? Maybe the name of a few churches?" asked Pastor Marshall.

"Not without their approval," Ted said quickly. "It's a privacy thing." He wasn't prepared to share any information about his business that could be investigated.

"I see," said Pastor Marshall. "Could you leave me your number so I can call you if I have any questions as I look over these suggestions?"

Ted said, "My contact information is on the back page."

After a few more questions, Ted and Alicia shook Pastor Marshall's hand and thanked him for his time.

After they left, Pastor Marshall looked over the list again and considered what these changes would cost and if they were, indeed, valid. He consulted his library, where he had kept a few books on church growth. He looked through them for church growth ideas that might correspond to those on the list. He had a lot of research to do before he could make any kind of decision.

Pastor Marshall, knowing that changes of this magnitude shouldn't be made alone, called a meeting of the elder board to share with them what had happened and to consider some of the changes that were in the list. He had studied up on church growth from his library and decided that some, if not all, of the suggestions had some merit.

The elder board met on Tuesday evening. All were present, except for Claude Nelson, who was on vacation. The meeting was called to order in the usual manner.

Pastor Marshall told them about his meeting with Ted and Alicia. There were questions about Ted and Alicia that no one could answer. No one knew them or had heard of them. It was suggested that someone needed to do some investigation to see what they could find out.

Henry Newgent knew the police chief and said that he would try to find out something through him. Nash Franks had made copies of the list and distributed them to everyone present. As they looked over the list, there was some discussion about the possibility of each suggestion. The church had some funds they could use for these suggestions, but there were questions about the need to spend for church growth. They were already one of the most attended churches in the area, but some were saying that if some of these suggestions were followed, they may increase attendance even more and could become the largest church in town. This idea seemed to put a smile on some of the elders' faces.

Pastor Marshall said, "Guys, let's be careful to not lose sight of our purpose here. We are not in the business of entertainment or marketing strategies for numerical growth. We are to be about the Lord's work in serving the community."

"That's all well and good, Pastor Marshall, but we also have to consider evangelism," said Bud Spear. "If we don't continually work to get them in church, they will never hear the gospel."

Pastor Marshall quickly responded, "Evangelism is not supposed to happen inside the church. It's supposed to happen outside the church. Once they are introduced to Jesus, then they are supposed to be ushered into the church to join us as the family of God."

Bud said, "But you're so much better at that than we are, Pastor."

"I'm not better or worse at it than you are," said Pastor Marshall. "I've trained you to share your faith. Each one of us has our own coming-to-faith story to share and we all touch different people in different ways."

The Elders all just looked at each other, knowing he was right.

Pastor Marshall continued, "If I decide to make changes, I would like you all behind me. So could I please ask each of you to take this list home and look it over? Consider each suggestion and ask yourself if this is what our church needs and pray to God for wisdom in our decision making. We can convene next week to continue with our discussion."

All agreed to consider their options and pray.

Henry Newgent made it over to the police station the next day to speak with the chief.

"Hey, Chief, do you have a minute to chat?"

"I always have time for my buddy Henry," said the chief. "Come to my office and let's chat. What's on your mind, Henry?"

"Well, Pastor Marshall had a visit from a new couple in town, the Wilsons, and we just don't know anything about them."

The chief said, "Well, why don't you just ask them who they are?"

"Well, none of us have ever seen them, and we don't have an address, or we would go visit them."

"Why do you want to know about them, Henry? Are they prospects for your congregation?"

"No, not really," said Henry. "You see, they came by to visit Pastor Marshall and suggested we make a lot of changes for church growth, and we just don't know anything about them."

"Are their names Ted and Alicia?" asked the chief.

"That's their names, why?"

"Well, Father Greene from Holy Cross was in here asking the same questions for the same reason. Seems they visited Father Greene with the same, or at least a similar, list. I told him I would ask around. I guess I had better get with it. I'll let you know what I find out."

Henry thanked the chief and was on his way.

The following Tuesday evening, the Elders Board met again for their regularly scheduled meeting. After Nash Franks had called them to order, Henry announced that he had met with Chief Peters but had not heard anything back about the investigation into the Wilsons. Pastor Marshall was disappointed but pressed forward with the meeting.

"We still don't know anything about who Ted Wilson is, or if these suggestions will do us any good. But until we know more, let's just look at these and decide for ourselves if we want to embrace any of them for our church," said Pastor Marshall.

All agreed, and they started with their questions about the list.

Claude was back from vacation and knew nothing of what had transpired the previous week.

Nash Franks told him, "There was a guy that came by last week and met with Pastor Marshall about some changes we should make to increase church attendance. It's all here on this list. We were asked to go home and look them over and pray for wisdom. We're back here tonight to start the discussions."

Claude thought it all weird, but he started reading through the list to see what all was there.

Nash suggested they go down the list by number and see if there needed to be any discussion of any item. Everyone agreed that Eric had a good idea. The first item was exterior upgrade to brick or stucco. Claude wanted to know what was wrong with the way the current church looked. Yes, it was metal and looked like a business building, but why was that an issue?

Pastor Marshall suggested, "I think what it's referring to is that the more 'inviting' the church looks, the more people it might attract."

Claude said, "Fair enough, I guess."

"How much do you think that would cost?" asked Nash.

Bud spoke up. "About twenty-five thousand dollars to do it in stucco."

"That's a lot of money to spend on appearance, don't you think?" asked Nash.

"It is," said Henry. "But if it will get more people here, it might be worth it."

The next item the Elder Board wanted to discuss was number 5, which was to landscape the whole complex.

Nash said, "It would be nice to have green grass that was edged around the drive and the sidewalk, and maybe even a playground in the back for the kids."

"Yes," Claude said. "My grandkids always get so dirty when they go out to play after church. All we have back there is dirt."

Bud said, "Need to add another twenty thousand dollars for all that."

As the meeting was drawing to a close, three items had been discussed: 1) exterior upgrade, 2) landscaping the complex, and 3) change of church colors and logo. Only the first page of the five-page document was looked at before the meeting exceeded its time.

Pastor Marshall said, "This is taking much longer than I thought it would to go through all these items. Currently, we are looking at only three items from this list, and the cost would be approximately sixty thousand dollars to complete. Now we should question whether or not we should do it."

Eric said, "Pastor, I suggest we sleep on it and continue to pray for wisdom. That's a lot of money for a facelift."

Pastor Marshall agreed. "Let's pray hard about spending money to basically buy church members."

"Pastor," Henry said, "I don't see it as 'buying' church members but, rather, improving the place we come to celebrate—and we do want others to join us."

"I can't argue with that, Henry. Let's just make sure we are all of that mindset—one that says we are making improvements for some other reason than church growth alone. See you guys next week."

And the pastor dismissed them with a prayer.

New Life Church

A few streets over from Dauphy's Diner stands a relatively new church that was started about two years earlier by a group from out of state. They thought that Faithville needed a church like theirs, so they gathered a group of people from a larger church in Tennessee and moved to South Georgia to start one. They had rented space at the local middle school and had broken ground to build their current building just a few months later. They have been in their new building for about a year now.

Their pastor is Reverend Jane Stewart, whom they call Reverend Jane. She is a middle-aged woman, of medium height and with dark hair, and is very friendly. She has been their leader from the beginning and has done a fine job keeping everyone together. They also suffer from low funds and low attendance.

During one of the regularly scheduled church services, Ted and Alicia were noticed in the congregation by Reverend Jane. After the service, Reverend Jane watched them visit with the other church members and went over to greet them.

"Hi there. I'm Reverend Jane."

"And we are the Wilsons. I'm Ted, and this is my wife, Alicia."

"So good to meet you and so excited that you chose to worship here with us today," said Reverend Jane.

"We are excited to be here and were wondering if you might have a chance to visit with us sometime this week?" asked Ted. "Well, do you have lunch plans?" asked Reverend Jane. Ted looked at Alicia, and they both smiled.

"We don't have any lunch plans," said Ted.

"Well, then, let's go grab a bite and we can meet there," said Reverend Jane.

They made their way to their cars and headed out. They met at Dauphy's Diner. After they shared some small talk, they placed their orders and continued visiting.

"Where are you from?" asked Reverend Jane.

Alicia said, "We are from a little town in Arkansas. We moved here to find new work about three months ago."

"Oh," said Reverend Jane. "What kind of work are you looking for?"

Ted said, "I do consulting, advertising, and marketing for big businesses. At least that's what I was doing. I'm wanting to scale down a little and just do medium- to small-sized businesses from now on."

"That's great! I'll keep my eyes and ears open and let you know if I hear anything," said Reverend Jane.

As the small talk ended and the food was served, Reverend Jane asked the Lord to bless their time together and the food they were to partake of. Then she asked, "So how may I be of assistance to you?"

Again, Ted and Alicia looked at each other and smiled.

"It's not how you can help us but how we can help you!" said Ted.

"Oh," said Reverend Jane. "And how do you want to help me?"

"We can help you grow your church!" said Ted and Alicia together.

"Okay. And how do you propose to do that?" asked Reverend Jane.

Just like with the other two church leaders, Ted and Alicia started excitedly talking about changes that could be made to the property and to the service that would attract more people.

Reverend Jane continued to eat her lunch and let them ramble on for about five minutes or so. She had completed her lunch before Ted and Alicia stopped talking. She Jane began to laugh.

Ted asked, "What's so funny?"

Reverend Jane apologized for laughing and said, "You just sounded like you had rehearsed all that to such a degree that you could have made a commercial."

And they all laughed. Ted said, "It's not a commercial, really, but I guess I could make one. I've been studying church growth for quite a while, and I know that if these suggestions are followed, your attendance will at least double in size over the next six months."

"Really?" asked Reverend Jane. "Can you put that in writing?" They all laughed.

As they paid for their food and exited the diner for their cars, Reverend Jane asked, "Can you put all those suggestions in writing and send me a copy? Here's my card, and my email address is on the bottom."

Ted said, "Sure thing. I'm excited to work on the details with you as soon as you're ready, Reverend Jane."

"Well, I would like to bounce these ideas off my Advisory Committee before I move any farther ahead," said Reverend Jane. "I am the decision maker for the church, but I've found it wise to seek approval from other concerned parties before making any financial decisions."

Ted had a scowl on his face, so Alicia said, "We understand that."

They shook hands, thanked each other for the time together, and departed.

Chief Peters had been at the diner for lunch and saw Reverend Jane in a meeting and was curious if maybe she was also meeting with the Wilsons. His waitress was the same one that served Reverend Jane's table, so when the waitress returned, he asked her, "Do you by chance know the names of the couple that was eating with Reverend Jane?"

The waitress said, "I think the last name was *Wilson* or *Williams*, I'm not sure."

"Thank you, sweetheart," said the chief as he paid his bill and left.

When Reverend Jane returned home, she brewed herself a cup of tea and started praying for wisdom. The idea of making changes was scary, but the idea of church growth was terribly appealing. She was the sole decision maker for the church, and she took that responsibility very seriously. She wanted to please God with every decision she made, and yet she wanted the church to be seen as alive and thriving. It was about two in the afternoon, so she called a meeting of the Advisory Committee, and they met the next evening.

"Thank you all for coming on such short notice. We had a couple of visitors at our service yesterday, so I went over to meet them. They asked if we could meet for a conversation, so I took them to lunch. Their names are Ted and Alicia Wilson. The meeting was a bit strange. You see, he and his wife have suggested they can help us grow the church. He sent me a list last night of things we can do to improve our facilities and services to make that happen. It's quite a long list. I've made copies for you all. Please take one and have a look."

All the committee members took one and started looking through it. Edna Rimes said, "Are these people legitimate? I mean, is this his profession?"

Reverend Jane said, "He has worked in the field of consulting, advertising, and marketing for big businesses, but he assured me that these same ideas will work for church growth."

Bob Taylor asked, "Is there money in the building fund for these updates?"

"Well," said Patricia Stanzer, who is also the church treasurer, "there's less than ten thousand dollars in there right now, but yesterday's offering isn't included. We usually get two hundred to three hundred dollars toward the building fund each week."

Edna said, "Some of these changes make good sense to me."

"I think they look great!" Freddy Sims said. "And think about it, we could have lots more people in the church on Sunday."

Reverend Jane said, "We have to be smart about this. We don't want to put our people in debt over something that's not going to work. Sure, we can make updates, and that is all well and good, but if we put our people in debt, they will not be happy if there is no return on our investment."

"I think you are speaking wisdom, Reverend Jane," said Bob. "We are not wealthy people."

They all agreed.

Reverend Jane said, "May I suggest, then, that we continue our discussion and meet again before I make any decisions? In the meantime, I will try to get more information on the Wilsons. It's just kind of strange to me that a new visitor would come in and want to start making changes. On the other hand, if a stranger who is into growing companies noticed that some changes could help us grow, well, that would be a gift to us.

"Let's meet again in a few days. I'll send out an email to you all with the time and date. I will also see what the rates are for a loan and maybe look into a capital campaign."

Bob said, "I can tell you right now, Reverend Jane, I like the sound of this, and I can't wait to start. On page 2, he's suggesting some changes to the service that look really exciting!"

Reverend Jane said, "I'll have to admit, I'm excited about all this as well!"

After a few days of trying to find any information on the Wilsons, Reverend Jane decided to visit Chief Peters at the police station. He should know something. She called the station to make sure he was in and asked for a meeting. They said he could see her now if that was convenient for her. She said she would be there in ten minutes, so off she went.

As Reverend Jane entered the police station, Chief Peters greeted her with a handshake and a cup of hot tea.

"I know you like tea, so I had them brew you a cup."

"That was so sweet of you," said Reverend Jane as they entered the chief's office.

Chief Peters asked, "What can I do for you today, Reverend Jane?"

"Well, this past Sunday, I had lunch with Ted and Alicia Wilson—"

The chief interrupted, "And they gave you a list of suggestions that you could do to increase your church growth?"

Reverend Jane looked shocked and said, "How did you know that, Chief Peters?"

"Well, it seems that he did the same thing with Father Greene at Holy Cross and Pastor Marshall at Freedom Church. The guy has made his rounds," said Chief Peters.

"Oh my!" said Reverend Jane. "Do you know anything about this couple?"

"All I know is that he now owns Jake Miller's farm because of some small print in a contract, so you need to watch yourself," said the chief. "It was all legal, and he was within his rights, but it just sounds a bit shady to me."

This was not what Reverend Jane wanted to hear. She liked the ideas that Ted had presented and was excited about the possibilities these changes held for the church. The idea that they could have lots of people in their church made her pride soar. But what would be the cost?

Oh well, she thought, *we will be sure to read everything carefully.*

The Advisory Committee met again on Thursday evening. Reverend Jane started the meeting by asking if anyone had any questions about the list of suggestions, the meeting from last week, or anything else.

There were no questions raised, so she continued, "I think we should look positively at the list. The changes will help with church growth, and even if it doesn't, let's ask ourselves, would it boost the morale of the people to see changes being made? Will they get involved in the changes that they have invested money in? And, if there's not church growth at all, will it still be a valid change?"

Bob spoke first. "We need to make some of these changes anyway, so I say we just bite the bullet and do it."

Everyone was in agreement, so Reverend Jane decided to move forward with the changes, which meant there would need to be a church meeting to present the changes, and the church would have to vote and decide by majority vote. The regularly scheduled meeting was this Sunday after the morning service. This would be a turning point for the church. Either the church would receive it as a wonderful idea or reject it as a waste.

Chapter

THREE

THE LEADERSHIP

Holy Cross Church

Back at Holy Cross Church, all the council was gathered for the meeting. Father Greene stood before them prepared for a discussion about the priorities of the church parish. The question had been put before the council at their last meeting: Why do people go to church?

Father Greene said, "Before we get tangled with questions about *if* we should do something, I think it would be wise for us to question why we go to church, and if that's the right question to ask. Though it seems that I'm talking in circles, let me assure you that I am not. You see, sometimes we do things just because they have always been done that way and we forget *why* we do them. For instance, why do we say the Apostle's Creed or the Nicene Creed in every service? Because with these words, we affirm our faith, and we continually affirm our faith so we won't forget it. There is a reason for it. In fact, in our tradition, we always have a reason for everything we do."

Father Greene continued, "Let's start first by asking, what is church? Well, church is not the building, and church is not just our people. The church is the entire body of Christ—those of our faith tradition and of other faith traditions. We are all one body in Christ. So why we go to church is probably not the question to be asking. Instead, maybe we should ask why we meet together as the Body of Christ?

"Consider that there was a disaster, maybe a hurricane or a tornado," Father Greene said. "There's no electricity, no food, no transportation, and no buildings. Everything was destroyed in the disaster. Would we meet? I hope your answer is yes. So if we meet, where would we meet?"

Someone laughed and said, "Dauphy's Diner."

Someone else said, "No diner. It was destroyed in the disaster."

Eric said, "I guess we could meet under a tree on Cal Jordan's farm."

Father Greene said, "Excellent idea. And what would we do when we meet?"

After a few moments of silence, Peter spoke up. "I assume we would pray, sing some songs, and hear some encouraging words from you, Father Greene."

"Yes," said Father Greene.

"And isn't that what we do on Sunday mornings?" Bud said.

"Yes, it is," Father Greene said. "And that is worship. We come together to worship."

"So," continued Father Green, "if the answer is not to worship, then we have the wrong answer. You see, God is the Maker of the Universe. God made everything that is and everything that will be. He's our Provider, the Giver of Grace, and for that alone, we owe Him our worship. That is first and foremost."

Father Greene continued, "We also fellowship, praise, serve, and other things, but worship is the centerpiece of church life. We gather to worship, and all these other things are a development of that worship. But sometimes we forget who we are worshiping, and just like the exiled Hebrews, after some time has passed, we begin to worship the golden calf. It's not because we want to but because we forget. I want to remind you that we must be guardians, not of just our own faith, but of the church faith. When we make decisions, it is my prayer that all decisions will be made believing that God comes before man. Is that decision glorifying God, or is it glorifying us?"

With that, Father Greene finished his talk, and the meeting was called to order by Eric.

Larry said, "Father Greene, I want to thank you for reminding us about worship. I lost my dad a couple years ago, and I remember feeling lost and lonely. The only place I felt a sense of peace was at church. And it's true that we are a family, but we are a spiritual family. It's not the fellowship or fun we have that brought me peace. No, it was the feeling, for me, that Christ dwells here. I know He dwells in our hearts as believers, but I think He also dwells in this place, where I worship Him."

"Thank you for that, Larry," said Father Greene.

Sammy agreed with Larry. "I know what you mean, Larry. Sometimes when we are taking communion, I feel extremely close to God. And when I eat His body and drink His blood, I can feel Him inside me. It's like His blood flows with mine."

"Exactly!" said Father Greene.

"Okay," said Eric, "we need to get down to business and look at this list with our new eyes. What do we want to discuss concerning painting the church?"

Leon said, "I can get scaffolding from my cousin Ned to use during the weekends and anytime he doesn't have jobs lined up. If we can get enough help, we can paint it ourselves, and we will only need to spring for the paint."

"Great idea, Leon," said Eric.

"Sammy, can you get us a discount on paint from your friends down at the paint store?" asked Eric.

"I'll do my best," said Sammy.

"Has anyone looked to see what's under the carpet in the sanctuary? Is it wood or cement?" asked Edward.

"I looked last week," said Pete. "It's wood. All we must do is move the pews out, rip up the carpet, sand the wood, and put on some wood sealer and we will have a brand-new wood floor! Okay, maybe a newly refinished floor."

"Sammy," said Eric, "can you add some sealer to your list for the paint store?"

"Sure can."

Eric said, "We should be able to complete those two items for roughly $3,500 if Sammy can get us a discount."

"I can talk to the men's and women's groups to see if we can set up a church fundraiser to raise that," said Eric.

So as the meeting continued, excitement began to show through the smiles on their faces. Holy Cross Church was going to get a facelift while they worked together as a family for the glory of God.

Freedom Church

Pastor Marshall was late for the elder meeting by about ten minutes because of a train. When he arrived, everyone was in a cheery mood. They had started without him, which made him feel as though he had been sidestepped. They had already gone down the list and decided on a few things without his input, and it didn't look as though they were going to even acknowledge that he was there.

Pastor Marshall said, "Would someone like to catch me up on what has been covered so far?"

Claude said, "Pastor, we have already gone over the first few items that we had previously talked about and decided to move forward with them."

"Well, wait a minute. What do you mean decided to move forward with them? You are not the decision makers, you're my sounding board. I called you together to help me make the decisions."

"And we did, Pastor. We decided to move forward," Nash said.

"You're not understanding me, Nash. I am the final decision maker for the church. That's why I was hired, and that's what's written in my job description."

Henry, who had been running the meeting, said, "Pastor, we didn't mean to overstep. We just talked about the items and decided we like most of them and we have the money to do them, so why not?"

"Well, I was hoping we could come to that final decision together before we decided to move forward with anything," said Pastor Marshall.

Bud said, "What's there to talk about? There was an item suggested, we discussed it and decided we think we should do it, so we marked it to do and moved on to the next one. We've already decided on four projects."

By this time, Pastor Marshall was pretty sure that things were out of hand. It was within his rights to dismiss the meeting if he thought it was out of hand, but what about the repercussions? What if they thought he was pulling rank?

So he said, "Just for a few minutes, could we please revisit the first item that you have already agreed on and ask ourselves *why* we are deciding to do it?"

"Pastor, with all due respect, we've already spent time talking about it. Let's just do it," said Nash.

Pastor Marshall said, "I'm not against doing any of these. I just want to make sure, and I want you to make sure, we are doing these things for the right reason."

Bud said, "The reason is that we want more people to come to our church. It seems simple to me that if we make these changes, Ted Wilson said it would increase our attendance. So let's do it!"

Pastor Marshall was about frantic at this point. He said, "Okay. Just answer one question about this first item: Are we doing this for us, or for God?"

Claude said, "That's an easy one, Pastor. We're doing this for God, because everyone knows that God wants more people to come to church. And if it's just money keeping us from them, then let's shell out the money and get them in here."

"Yes," everyone except Pastor Marshall said.

He knew the meeting was out of control now, so he pulled the trump card and said, "This meeting is adjourned."

And he left, assuming everyone else would too. But they didn't. They stayed and continued going through the list. They stayed another two hours, in fact, and finished the whole list. When they had finished, they had all agreed to twelve projects, with a total cost of roughly two hundred thousand dollars.

Each Elder was assigned a task to get done as soon as possible. There were bankers to talk to, the finance committee, someone needed to find Ted Wilson, and they needed to find some people with money to donate. Everyone was happy, and there was new energy in their mission. They were going to prepare for a full church in the very near future.

When Pastor Marshall got home, he was exhausted and so very frustrated. There was a message on his answering machine, so he listened to it. It was a message from Henry Newgent saying that the chief had called with some information about Ted Wilson, but he had only received a voice message, so he didn't know what the chief had found out. He decided to pay a visit to Chief Peters first thing in the morning.

Pastor Marshall was at the police station at seven. The chief didn't get there until about seven thirty, so he waited. As soon as the chief arrived, he saw Pastor Marshall and said, "Well, hello, Pastor Marshall! What brings you to the station?"

They greeted each other with a handshake, and Pastor Marshall said, "I was just wondering if I could talk to you privately?"

"Of course," Chief Peters said. "Let's go to my office."

In the office, Pastor Marshall said, "Henry told me you had some information for us about Ted Wilson."

"Yes, I do," Chief Peters said. "I followed him home from the diner on Sunday and saw that he's living at the old Miller place. I didn't know if he bought it or was just renting it, so I called Jake Miller. Jake said that the Wilsons cheated him out of his farm."

Pastor Marshall said, "What?"

"Yes. He said it was supposedly all legal because of some small print that Jake didn't read. He got a loan from Ted, and when he was late on his second note, the farm went into foreclosure. It was a scam. But there was nothing poor Jake could do."

"That's terrible," said Pastor Marshall. "Is Jake, and his family, okay?"

31

Chief Peters said, "They had to move in with their kids, but they said they would be okay."

"Is there anything that can be done about that?"

"I'm afraid not. I called Chester Quave, who is a lawyer, and asked him about it. He had heard of it and had already pulled the files. There's nothing anyone can do because Jake signed on the dotted line."

Pastor Marshall said, "This is a serious matter because he's the guy that gave us a list of suggestions for church growth, and our elders are all for making the changes without my approval. This Ted Wilson has them all in a stir."

"Not just your church," Chief Peters said. "He also made a visit to Father Greene at Holy Cross. And Ted and Alicia Wilson were having lunch with Reverend Jane from over at New Life Church. This guy has been busy. Keep your eyes open, Pastor. I believe this guy may be one of the black sheep."

New Life Church

The church service ended, and it was announced that the regularly scheduled church business meeting was to proceed, so nonmembers were dismissed. Reverend Jane's hands were sweaty, and she was nervous about what was about to take place. As everyone quieted down, she walked to the front and tapped the microphone to be sure it was on.

She cleared her throat and said, "Thank you all for staying for our meeting. I promise it will not be long. Then we can all head over to Dauphy's."

Everyone laughed, but they all knew that sometimes these business meetings could get lengthy and violent.

Reverend Jane opened the meeting with prayer asking God to watch over them and to help them to always keep Him first. The minutes from the last business meeting were read. There were no questions, and they were voted on and approved. After they determined that there weren't any old business, they moved on to the new business.

"There is some new business that has come up that I want to share with you," said Reverend Jane. "A couple weeks ago, we had a couple of visitors, so I invited them to lunch so we could get to know each other. In that time together, Ted Wilson made some suggestions that would supposedly increase our chances for church growth. He presented me with a list, which we have copied for you and is being distributed now. If you didn't get one, please hold up your hand."

The ushers handed out the copies of the list.

"I met with my Advisory Committee a couple times already to discuss and pray for wisdom. And we have decided to move forward with a few of these items, so we bring them now before you to get your approval and partnership.

"As you look down the list, just raise your hand or speak out, and the committee and I will field the questions."

A question came from the middle of the room: "Which of these items did you decide on?" It was Edna.

"If you notice, there's an asterisk right after the item number that signifies the ones we thought were important."

Ruffus Haines asked, "Why did you just choose some and not all of them? If this guy knows it will work, should we just do them all?"

Patricia said, "We were thinking about the cost. If we do them all, it's a lot of money, possibly one hundred thousand dollars or so. The ones we chose would total about forty-five thousand dollars."

Vance Cuzak, the banker in town, said, "It's been my experience that if you halfway do something, it's more liable to fail. I think if we do this, we should do it all."

A large number of those present said, "Yes! Do it all."

Reverend Jane had a smile on her face. She was excited that there was such support. "Would you all be interested in starting a capital fundraising campaign to get all this done?" she asked.

There was a resounding "Yes!" from the whole group. There was excitement in the air.

"Okay," said Reverend Jane. "I must admit I'm quite excited about this too. I have reached out to a company that handles capital fundraising, so I will meet with them next week. But before that, we need to have a vote, by a show of hands, for the church minutes. All in favor of moving forward with the whole list, please raise your hands."

Pretty much the whole group raised their hands.

The reverend continued, "All those opposed by the same sign."

And there were none. So, by majority vote, the church had decided to move forward with the whole list.

Chapter

FOUR

THE THREE

Once things had settled down, the church leaders were thinking about the direction they were currently headed. Each church is different, and so is each leader. Some churches give all power to one person, while others require boards, committees, or councils to help give direction; but pretty much all churches are governed by the people when it comes to big decisions like spending money from the church budget.

Churches usually choose a leader based on credentials, past experiences, manner of relating to people, etc. But mainly, it's about love for God and the ability to lead the church in a godly direction.

Father Greene was educated in a seminary, had served three prior churches with good rapport, loved the people and had been a faithful steward in leading them with godly conviction, yet he was a mild-mannered man. Pastor Marshall was educated in a public university, had led businesses, was a great speaker, loved the people, and wanted to please God with all his heart. He had proven to be a good leader and had strong convictions about the church being a godly place. Reverend Jane had been to a community college and had earned an associate of arts degree. She was a lovely person who publicly professed Christ as her Savior with no hesitation. She loved the church and wanted the best for it.

Pastor Marshall knew that things were getting out of hand at Freedom Church, and he knew he needed to do something pretty quickly. As he racked his brain trying to think of something, he remembered his conversation with Chief Peters. Ted Wilson visited at least two other church leaders besides himself. He wondered what they were doing with the list.

Maybe it's time for a meeting of the leaders, he thought.

Early the next morning, Pastor Marshall called Holy Cross Church.

Mrs. Alexander answered the phone.

"Hi, Mrs. Alexander, this is Pastor Marshall from Freedom Church. Is Father Greene in?"

"Well, hello there, Pastor Marshall," Mrs. Alexander said. "He's in, let me see if he's available to talk."

She buzzed Father Greene's office. He was free to talk. "He'll be right with you, Pastor Marshall," said Mrs. Alexander.

"Hello, Pastor Marshall," said Father Greene. "How can I help you?"

"Father Greene, thanks for taking my call. I heard that you had a visit with Ted Wilson a few weeks ago and was wondering if maybe we could meet sometime soon to chat about that?"

"I would be delighted to," said Father Greene. "Your place or mine?"

"Well, I'm not sure yet. I also wanted to invite Reverend Jane from New Life Church. She too had a visit with the Wilsons. I was going to call her next," said Pastor Marshall.

Father Greene said, "Just let me know when and where and I'll be there."

"Thank you, Father Greene," said Pastor Marshall.

As soon as he hung up, the pastor called New Life Church. After a brief chat with Reverend Jane, they agreed to meet the following evening at Dauphy's. Pastor Marshall then informed Father Greene.

The next evening, the three church leaders met at Dauphy's. They ordered decaf coffee and then began to discuss the Wilsons and their suggestion list. They each brought a copy to compare. What they noticed was that the lists were very similar, maybe even the same, just reworded and with the items in a different order. It appeared that maybe there was just one list but put into three lists that looked different.

"That's weird," said Father Greene. "These lists are actually the same. They weren't created based on our churches. They are just general church growth ideas."

"I agree," said Pastor Marshall.

Reverend Jane said, "Isn't it interesting how every entry could be construed as 'needed' at possibly every church?"

Father Greene and Pastor Marshall both agreed. "Why would he do that?" asked Pastor Marshall.

"I don't know," said Father Greene. "I think we haven't heard the last of the Wilsons. We need to be on our guard."

They agreed that they should call some other churches to see if they'd had any contact with the Wilsons. They divided up a list of all the churches in town for each to call. After they had made their calls, they would contact one another with their findings.

It didn't take long to make the calls. What they found was they were the only three churches that were contacted by the Wilsons. Why would Holy Cross, Freedom, and New Life be the only churches they were persuading to invest in church growth? That just didn't seem to make any sense. If this was some kind of scam, no one could see how it worked. They met back at Dauphy's Diner to share what they had found.

Pastor Marshall asked, "Have any of you shared this with your decision-making groups?"

Both Father Greene and Reverend Jane said yes.

"And where are you in that process?" asked Pastor Marshall.

Father Greene spoke first. "We have decided to ignore church growth and let God choose who comes to Holy Cross. Instead, we chose to look at the list as a to-do list and make the upgrades or changes suggested on the list based on whether or not we feel it's something that needs done, solely for the glory of God."

"What about your church, Reverend Jane?" asked Pastor Marshall.

"Well, I have an Advisory Committee that I met with, and the suggestion from them was that we move forward with a lot of the items on the list, but not all, because we didn't want to put the church in debt. And I must say there was quite a bit of excitement thinking our church might grow from this. I must admit that I was excited myself. This past Sunday, we had our regularly scheduled church business meeting, so I brought it up. To my surprise, the church voted to do the entire list! We will start a capital campaign to raise the funds. Everyone was excited, and the vote was unanimous!"

Father Greene asked, "And, Pastor Marshall, what about your church? Where are they?"

Pastor Marshall looked sad. He said, "I met with our Elder Board. Well, actually, I was a few minutes late for the meeting and they started without me."

"That's never good," said Father Greene.

"No, it's not," said Pastor Marshall. "Before I got there, they had already decided what they wanted to do. There was no talking to them about what God might want or what is good for our people or our budget. They just talked over me, like I wasn't even there."

"Oh my!" said Reverend Jane. "I'm so sorry. I will remember you and your church in my prayers."

"As will I," said Father Greene.

"I'm just so confused about why our churches and no others were given this list. There has to be something we're missing," said Pastor Marshall.

Just then, they noticed Chief Peters enter the Diner. They motioned for him to come over to their table.

"Chief Peters, we were wondering if you would join us for a few minutes," said Father Greene.

"Well, sure," said Chief Peters.

"We were meeting tonight to talk about the list that was given to us by the Wilsons," said Father Greene.

Reverend Jane said, "We have made some calls and found that we are the only three churches in town that received the list. And we found that the lists are all the same, just reworded and with the items rearranged."

"We don't know if it's a scam. And if it's a scam, we don't see the angle," added Pastor Marshall.

The chief just looked puzzled. "I wish there was something I could do to help."

Pastor Marshall asked, "Is it possible to do a background check?"

"Well, yes," said Chief Peters. "But you would have to notify Mr. Wilson that he is being investigated. I don't think you want that just yet."

"No," said Pastor Marshall.

Chief Peters said, "Maybe you should all get on the internet and do your own search. There are some sites that will provide you all kinds of information, and there are some sites that will scam you, so be careful."

"That's a good idea," said Pastor Marshall.

Chapter

FIVE

THE MEETING

Holy Cross Church

Meetings were coming up in all three of the churches that were given the list. Holy Cross met on Tuesday evening. The people were friendly, as they always were.

Father Greene addressed the crowd. "Good evening, friends. It's that time again, so we meet to take care of our church's business. I will lead you in prayer, then our good brother Eric will take it from there."

Father Greene led them in prayer asking for wisdom and vision as they took care of the business of their parish. And there was a hearty "Amen" that followed.

Eric called the meeting to order. After a vote to receive the minutes from the last meeting, they moved on to the old business. The only old business was an issue with the spelling of Father Greene's name on the website. Eugene Reynolds promised he would fix it as soon as he could. Then they moved on and asked if there was new business.

Eric said, "Father Greene has some new business he would like to share.

Father Greene returned to the front of the parish and spoke. "A couple visited our parish on Sunday morning about a month ago and asked if they could meet with me. I invited them to my office, and they presented me with a list of suggestions for our church. They said these changes would improve our chances for church growth. I have shared that list with the church council. We have looked over the list and have decided that it would be in the best interest of the parish to do just those things on the list that would need to be done. This way, we are not looking for church growth but merely hoping that God will bless us for our efforts."

Someone in the back of the group asked, "What else was on the list?"

Someone else asked, "Can we see the list?"

Father Greene said, "The list is quite extensive. We didn't think it would be a very good use of our time to go through the whole list with you because there are some items on it that the church council really didn't think appropriate."

Someone else asked, "Is there a reason you don't want us to see the list, Father Greene?"

"Not at all," replied Father Greene. "If you want to see the list, we can make copies for you."

A quick show of hands made Father Greene ask Mrs. Alexander to make copies for the people.

The copies were handed out, and the parishioners began reading through them and murmuring to themselves. It wasn't long before the questions started.

"Father Greene, which ones have you and the council decided we should do?"

"How much will this cost?"

"How long will it take to get them done?"

The questions continued for more than an hour. Father Greene and several church council members were fielding them. They had already spent countless hours poring over the list and were looking forward to this night ending.

Finally, a question from Billy Larkin: "Father Greene, why are we not making any of the changes suggested about the service? It seems to me that a lot of people might like adding electric guitars and drums to our service."

Father Greene had feared that these kinds of questions would come up if they were given the entire list. He said, "Our tradition is not opposed to the use of various instruments in our worship. However, there is a sense of reverence that we do adhere to pretty strictly when we enter into a place that is reserved for the worship of God. It would seem that it should be different from what the world is currently involved in. Many say we have to change with the times, and while that is true, in a sense, we have to keep the purpose of our meeting together for worship to be focused on pleasing God."

Billy said, "Are you suggesting that God doesn't like electric guitars?"

Father Greene said, "Billy, I believe that's the wrong question. One of my favorite movies is *Jurassic Park*, and in the first one, Dr. Malcolm makes a statement that is actually quite brilliant. He said, 'I'm paraphrasing: Your scientists were so preoccupied with whether they could they never stopped to consider if they should.' I think we have to ask if changing our service by shortening prayers and sermons, and maybe adding instruments, is a good thing. Would those changes be for our own pleasure or God's own pleasure? And if we make those changes, what are we saying to the community? Are we saying that we surrender to the world—we want to be like them?"

Eric interrupted, "Father Greene, I think maybe we need some reminders about our faith. Why do we come to worship? Why do we worship the way we do? What things are changeable, and what things aren't? I would suggest that maybe we could have a workshop on these things either by you or someone else."

Father Greene said, "That's a splendid idea!" I would love to do a workshop with you, and I suppose we could do that as early as next week."

Then it was agreed by all present that there would be a workshop next week to talk about the elements of our worship.

Father Greene was excited because he had always been fascinated by the liturgy of their tradition and had studied extensively in various denominational liturgies. Even the nontraditional churches had a liturgy whether they knew it or not, because liturgy means the work of the people. He began to consult his library on books of worship and found that he had quite a collection—a total of eighty-two books on the subject of worship alone. He had more books on the history, traditions, and sacraments of the church, but he didn't think he needed those at this point.

Oh, he thought. *This is going to be a very good thing for our church!*

Freedom Church

It was a chilly night as Pastor Marshall drove to the church on Wednesday evening. The monthly business meeting would be held in the sanctuary immediately following their midweek prayer service. He was very uneasy about the meeting. When the Elder Board met last week, they had acted as though he wasn't even there. They conducted the meeting without consulting him about anything. And now they had been afforded enough time to talk among themselves. And even though the elders were not supposed to talk to anyone about the meetings they had, in the past, too many people have known about meeting conversations to think they actually followed that rule.

Maybe it was paranoia, but Pastor Marshall detected that people were very complacent. They weren't making eye contact with him.

This is a bad sign, he thought.

All his attempts to liven them up failed. He felt like a fool trying to manipulate them into a good mood. When he asked if anyone had any praise reports or prayer requests, there was no response. Now he knew something was up because each week there were several reports and requests, but tonight there were none. He didn't linger with the service.

After the prayer service, Pastor Marshall announced, "Tonight is our monthly business meeting, so those of you who are not members of this congregation may please excuse themselves."

Pastor Marshall called the meeting to order and asked Penny, the church secretary, to read the minutes from the last meeting. Penny read the minutes, and Pastor Marshall asked if there were any additions or deletions. There were none. He asked for approval of the minutes, and everyone raised their hands. He asked for any disapprovals, and there were none.

"Is there any old business?" asked Pastor Marshall.

There was none.

"Any new business?"

Claude Nelson made his way to the front of the church with his notes in hand.

Pastor Marshall said, "Claude, do you have new business?"

Claude said, "Yes, I do."

"I wasn't informed that there was new business to be discussed. Our bylaws state that any new business to be discussed in business meetings must be approved by the pastor of the church."

Claude said, "It's okay, Pastor. It's just the things we agreed on in our board meeting."

Pastor Marshall said, "Claude, we didn't agree on anything in the board meeting."

Claude said, "You didn't, but we did. We've been talking about it all week, and we have made a decision of what we should do."

Pastor Marshall didn't like confrontation, especially not in front of others. He calmly said to Claude, "We can talk about this in my office tomorrow. It's not ready to go in front of the whole church."

Claude rebuked him, "No, Pastor Marshall, we have already made the decision, and it's going to the church tonight!"

"No, it's not," Pastor Marshall said in a much sterner tone. "I can call the meeting. Is that what you would like?"

Claude just wheeled around, grabbed a microphone, and started addressing the congregation. "Ladies and gentlemen, the board met last week to discuss a list of suggestions for church growth that was—"

And his microphone went silent. Pastor Marshall had signaled the audio tech to cut his microphone. As he did, the pastor spoke in his own microphone.

"I'm sorry, but the meeting is now over. I have the right to call the meeting whenever I feel it's out of hand, and right now, I feel that it's out of hand. Go home and have a good night."

Claude was angry. He turned to Pastor Marshall and said, "You had best be in your office in the morning at nine. The Elder Board will be paying you a visit."

Pastor Marshall said, "I'll be there, Claude. Now go home and have a good night."

New Life Church

New Life Church had their monthly meeting on the same night as Freedom Church. Reverend Jane was not worried about the meeting—in fact, she was looking forward to it. Though it was a chilly evening, she looked up at the evening sky and soaked up the beauty of the stars surrounding the brilliant moon. As she enjoyed the view, she said aloud, "God, You truly are the Master Creator!" Then she turned and walked inside.

The people were cheery and happy that night. They acted as though it was already Christmas and they were in their anticipation zone. Reverend Jane started greeting people as she made her way to the front. It was almost time for the meeting to start. Edna Rimes was already on the stage waiting for the reverend, motioning to her to come on. Reverend Jane excused herself from the conversation and headed quickly to the stage.

"Good evening, everyone!" said Reverend Jane. "Everyone just looks so happy and excited! Did I miss something? Somebody's birthday? I know, you're just so excited that it's finally time for our monthly business meeting, right?"

Everyone laughed and said, "Yeah, right!"

"Well, then," said Reverend Jane, "let's get this party started!"

Edna Rimes was head of the Advisory Committee and typically officiated the monthly business meetings. Edna called the business meeting to order. She asked if there was any old business.

Peter King said, "I don't think we ever came to a decision about the well. I don't care one way or the other, but we always seem to

47

push these things to the back burner, and nothing gets done. So are we going to fix it, or not?"

After a few minutes of discussion, the decision was made not to fix the old well but to fill it in with dirt.

"Any other old business?" asked Edna.

There was no other old business, so she moved on to the new business.

Regina Hartley came to the front of the church, took a microphone, and said, "The Ladies Auxiliary wants to do a yard sale on the church grounds. I have discussed this with Reverend Jane, and we didn't find any reasons that we shouldn't, so we bring that to the church body for a vote."

Edna said, "Any questions for Regina?"

A voice asked, "What are you selling, Regina?"

Regina said, "We are hoping that all of you would have some things in your closets or your garages that you don't need anymore. You could bring those things to the yard sale."

The same voice said, "Do we keep the money, or do you?"

A few people chuckled.

Regina said, "Well, the whole reason for having the yard sale is to provide more funds for the church building fund."

The same voice said, "That's a good idea. I was just asking."

A different voice asked, "Why are these proceeds going to the building fund? Are we building something?"

Regina said, "The building fund also serves as the maintenance fund. It should really be called the building and maintenance fund, but it's not. It's just called the building fund. Anyhow, it's used to build new things, but it's also used to maintain what we have." Then she said, "You never know when we might be building something." Then she turned and winked at Reverend Jane.

Reverend Jane just looked puzzled.

They voted to have the yard sale, and Edna asked for any other new business. No one spoke up, so Reverend Jane took center stage.

"If no one else has any new business, then I would like to share with you some new business. As you know, last meeting we voted to move forward with the suggestion list that I was given."

Everyone cheered.

Reverend Jane smiled and said, "I hope you're ready for an adventure! Because we are about to embark on an exciting journey of transformation. We are going to change the appearance and tradition of our church."

The crowd was excited, laughing and cheering!

"I had conversations with a couple of banks, and the interest rates are pretty high. I have talked with two capital campaign groups. One has called back favorably, and the other said it wouldn't be beneficial for them to work with us and wished us the best. So tonight I have asked our representative from the capital campaign company that called us back. His name is Johnathan Zahn. Please make him welcome."

Everyone gave a welcoming applause.

Johnathan said, "Please, call me John."

John was clean-cut and polished. He spoke well and was very convincing, even though the congregation at New Life Church needed no convincing. They had already made up their mind that they wanted to change and grow. At the end of John's presentation, there were a few questions, which were answered quickly.

Edna asked if there were any more questions, and there were none. So Reverend Jane said, "Okay, folks. This is real. Remember that you are already giving to our general fund. This campaign is asking you to go over and above what you already give to help us reach the goal we need. Do you all understand that?"

Everyone yelled, "Yes, we do!"

Everything got quiet. John read the proposal. Reverend Janet asked, "Does someone want to put this proposal that was just read to you in the form of a motion?"

Bob Taylor said, "I put this in the form of a motion."

Nancy Sullivan quickly gave a second.

Reverend Jane said, "Okay, all those in favor of this motion, please raise your hand."

It looked as though everyone raised their hand. Reverend Jane asked them to put their hands down after they were counted. Then she said, "All those not in favor, please raise your hand."

No hand went up. The vote to do the whole list and enter a huge fundraising season was unanimous!

When Reverend Jane got home, she made herself a cup of tea and sat back in her favorite chair to relive the recently concluded meeting.

It's amazing that a list of suggestions has caused so much excitement in our little church, she thought. *Amazing that there was no discord, no challenge. Could it be that God had His hand in this?*

She lingered with that thought for a while because she enjoyed it.

Then her mind changed. What if this was all a trick of the evil one? What if we were set up for a fall? Did we move too quickly? Before she got too deep in the what-ifs, she realized her cup was empty and said out loud, "Well, time for bed."

And she didn't allow herself to think about it anymore that night.

Chapter

SIX

HOLY CROSS WORKSHOP

Calendar

They gathered on Wednesday nights. Father Greene said, "The content of these talks could be talked about for years. But for you, I have trimmed them down to four weeks. We will have to move pretty quickly to get through the material. Just remember, we are only doing an overview because there's just too much material. At a later time maybe, we can do a more in-depth study on particular areas. But for now, we will be looking at these items for the four weeks: One, calendar. Two, Word. Three, sacrament. And four, music. All headed under the subject of worship."

As they took out their pads, pencils, pens, laptops, tablets, and phones, the teaching began. Father Greene explained how using the church calendar keeps us thinking about the story of Jesus all year round. Through each season we remember, we pray, we live with Christ. By walking with Him through the birth, the life, the crucifixion, the resurrection, and the ascension, it helps us to stay focused on Him and what He must have been thinking through these times. It also causes us to more deeply expect and anticipate His return.

He talked about the church year beginning the first Sunday of Advent. "To find the first Sunday of Advent, you go to Christmas Day and count four Sundays back. So there are four Sundays of Advent, then Christmas follows before the next Sunday. Advent is a time of preparation. It usually follows a nonstandardized theme so some churches may choose different themes. But our church uses hope, peace, joy, and love for those four Sundays. You will notice also that there are four candles circling a wreath—three purple and one pink. The pink one is a bit special because it is called the shepherd candle, or the candle of joy. And that Sunday, the third Sunday of Advent, is called Gaudete Sunday. It's the turning point in the Advent season. The first two weeks are marked as 'coming' and now, the third and fourth weeks are marked as 'He is near.'

"And finally, we make it to Christmas, the birth of our Lord, at which time the Christ Candle, which is the large white candle in the center of the wreath, is lit. But that's not all! Wait for it. He told them there really are twelve days of Christmas. You can celebrate them any way you like, but after the twelfth day of Christmas, we find ourselves at Epiphany on January 6. This is the manifestation of Christ to the Gentiles, as represented by the Magi arriving. Some may call it Magi Day, and others may call it Three Kings Day, but we know it as Epiphany.

"Next, we find ourselves in something called Ordinary Time. There are two great seasons of the church referred to as Christmastide and Eastertide. Ordinary Time is the season that falls outside those times and outside their preparatory seasons of Advent and Lent, respectively. So Ordinary Time falls after Christmas and before

Lent, and again after Pentecost and before Advent. We still follow the life of Christ through these lesser seasons with our scripture readings, prayers from the prayer book, and sermons, of course.

Then we shall find ourselves getting ready for Easter during the time of Lent. It begins on Ash Wednesday. And you may ask, when is Ash Wednesday? Ash Wednesday is the Wednesday preceding the first Sunday in Lent, and forty-six days before Easter. And you may ask, when is the first Sunday in Lent? That would be the Sunday following Ash Wednesday. And you may ask, when is Easter? Well, that's a bit more complicated. Easter is a movable feast, which means it doesn't have a particular date like Christmas on the twenty-fifth of December. Instead, its date is based on the moon. You see, Easter is the first Sunday after the full moon, after March 21. Yeah, I know, it's easier to just google it.

On Ash Wednesday, we mark our heads with ashes from last Easter's burning of the palm branches. The palm branches were blessed before the Easter Vigil, and it's our belief that anything blessed needs to be burned or buried. We burn them before Ash Wednesday so they can be used to mark our heads as reminders of what season is coming. Lent is coming!

"During Lent, things change. As we near the time of our Savior's death, we walk with Him in a way. We pray, we fast (abstain from things that distract us and focus more on God), and we give. It's a time of quietness and reflection. It's a time of getting our lives right, repenting and turning from sin, and looking forward to that great resurrection morning when Christ arose from the grave, victorious!

"Easter is the greatest Christian celebration because it was on that day that He arose and conquered death, hell, and the grave! We celebrate more on this day than any other Christian feast day.

"The Sunday following Easter is Pentecost Sunday. It marks the beginning of the season of Pentecost and lasts for fifty days. It was the time we received the gift of the Holy Spirit and saw the birth of the church."

The hour was growing late. There had been so many questions to answer that the time had just slipped away.

Father Greene said, "Sorry to cut this short, but we are out of time, so let me just say that after Pentecost, we find ourselves back to a new church year and, once again, the beginning of Advent."

He dismissed them with a prayer asking God to always hold them close and help them to remember why He is Love.

Word

The second workshop was on a particular part of the liturgy. Father Greene explained that the word *liturgy* means "the work of the people."

"Worship is something we do, so worship and liturgy are somewhat tied together, liturgy being the catalyst so to speak. You could look at our liturgy in at least two parts. They are Word and Sacrament, sometimes called Liturgy of the Word and Liturgy of the Table. Today we will cover Word, and next week, Sacrament. These things are all outlined in our prayer book from which we are guided.

"The Word section of the service refers to those things we do the first half of the service, including prayers, scripture readings, sermons, etc. If you will notice, there was no mention of music. Music is a supplement that doesn't have a section of its own because it is used throughout the entire service, not just a part. Because of that, it will be covered by itself in the fourth workshop.

"Soren Kierkegaard once made a statement that worship was like a drama or a theatrical play. He thought that other churches felt the same way, but they had taken on the wrong roles. They had God as the prompter. The leaders (musicians, readers, preachers, celebrants, etc.) had become the actors, and the congregation became the audience. The leaders thought they were better equipped to be the actors or performers, so the congregation should just watch. And many churches are still teaching this way. This way of thinking was wrong according to Kierkegaard. The leaders were to be the prompters, the congregation and the leaders were to share the role of actors or performers, and God alone is the audience.[1] This is the only way that makes sense, and our faith tradition has embraced it. That's why our worship is participatory—everyone participates.

"Any meeting has a beginning and an end. The same is true with the Word part of the service. We refer to the beginning of the Word part of the service as the Gathering, Entrance, Call to Worship, or some other name that assembles us together and gives us a starting point.

"Any meeting also has an ending. The same is true with the Sacrament section of our service. When the Sacrament section is over, we can't just go home, so we have a short dismissal or a sending forth to do the Lord's bidding, to share Christ with others, to live the Christ-filled life!

What happens in the Word section of our service? Well, we are called together to worship by any variety of ways. We could use scripture. We could use a song that by its text calls us together. Larger churches could have a procession. We could use a psalm chant. We could use a projected message on a screen, or we could simply pray

---

[1]   "Be a Part of Our Musical Worship Leadership", http://www.worshipand churchmusic.com/kierkegaard.html

that we attune our hearts to commune with Him. No matter which one we choose, we are gathered together as the people of God for the purpose of worshiping Him. There is a short prayer that segues us from Gathering to Word called the collect of the day. It gives us a hint of where the theme of the readings is pointing.

Typically, the whole of our worship is prayer. It gives credence to Paul's charge to pray without ceasing. There is a logical flow from one part to the next as we move through prayers, the readings (including Old Testament, Psalm, New Testament and Gospel, where we all participate), to the sermon, where the readings are explained. These readings are related to the Christian Calendar, which we discussed last week.

These readings are selected in a three-year cycle that covers all the major points in the Gospel so that after three years, we have covered them all, and we start all over again. These Sunday readings are all contained in our Lectionary—a big book containing all the readings. They are also listed in our prayer books for everyone—not only in our parish but in all the parishes that share our faith tradition. Now everyone has all the scripture readings for any given Sunday so they can read and meditate on them days or weeks before the service. The gospel passage is always the last reading before the sermon, and it's given special attention, with everyone standing.

"The sermon follows. This is where the presider, celebrant, preacher, orator, or speaker stands before the people to explain the scriptures that were read. If the speaker has studied well, he would be able to tie the scripture lessons to the Gospel reading and see how everything comes together, still relating to the current season in the church calendar.

"Following the sermon, we affirm our faith by reciting the Creed. We are taught that we should 'contend for the faith that was once for all delivered to the saints' as outlined in our prayer book. We use the Nicene Creed for our Sunday service, or Mass as it is called. The Nicene Creed was written when the church was undivided. The document was produced as an expansion of an earlier Apostle's Creed. By reciting this creed we affirm our faith and are reminded of the things we believe, to keep them near our hearts.

"Prayer is the language of our worship. These prayers are not just rote but are also valid for the day. The Prayers of the People follows the Creed. Here we are reminded to pray for broader things, from the universe all the way down to our personal daily needs, like food and shelter. It's a time where we add our own prayers and petitions aloud and silently.

"We cannot enter the second part of the service unclean, so there is a confession and absolution. We pray for the sins we've committed knowingly and unknowingly and ask God to forgive us and make us clean. The absolution is the reminder that when we confess our sins, God is faithful and just to forgive our sins and cleanse us from all unrighteousness. It's not a magical prayer, of course. We must repent, which means to refocus or change course. So if we are truly ashamed of our sins, we will leave that sin and change course.

The time, again, was running short, so Father Greene apologized for going overtime, but there were many questions to be answered. He continued by adding that the second part of the service was the Lord's Table.

"The scriptures remind us that taking the Lord's Supper in the wrong way could be detrimental, so if you have issues with your brother (or sister), then you should first go to them and make it right. So the final part of the Word section is called the Passing of the Peace. That's where we go to one another and say something like 'The peace of the Lord be with you,' and they respond, 'And also with you.' The thinking is that you can't have issues with someone and pass them peace. If there is an issue, this is the time to make amends, or please do not take communion."

After a couple more questions, they were dismissed with prayer. Father Greene prayed that the teachings shared this evening would remain in their hearts and minds as they sought to bring honor and glory to Him who made all things. Amen.

Sacrament

"Just a quick recap revealed that the first week, we talked about the Christian Calendar and how it keeps us connected to the life of Christ. Last week we talked about the first of the two parts of our service, Word. This week we will talk about the second part, the Sacrament. The Service of the Word and the Service of the Sacrament are both equally important. One does not take precedence over the other. They are done together to make a whole. And might it be added here that if you add the beginning and the ending, it is actually a fourfold service consisting of the Gathering, the Service of the Word, the Service of the Sacrament, and the dismissal.

"The second part of our service, the Service of the Sacrament, is like a response to everything that has happened in the first part of the service, the Service of the Word. Here we respond to the prayers, readings, and the sermon by giving of ourselves in praise, prayer, and communing with Him, then remembering to thank Him for feeding us with Himself.

"First, we give to Him our tithes and offerings as giving back of a portion of what He has blessed us with. We give from the heart, knowing that God will use these gifts to provide us a place to worship and carry out our mission here on earth to serve and provide for others less fortunate. There are no strings attached to what we give. It was His, for He has already provided that for us. We return a portion to Him to be used as He sees fit. We give out of love for Him.

The Eucharist is the formal name we give to the Lord's Supper. *Eucharist* means "great thanksgiving," and is that not what the Lord's Supper is? In it we remember His sacrifice—sacrificing His body and blood on that cruel cross to provide salvation for us. He shows us both grace and mercy because we are sinners. Wouldn't our natural response be a great 'Thank You!' to our Lord and King? Of course, it would.

"The prayers of the Eucharist bring focus to the fact that our Lord instituted this act to commune with Him together as His people. We are part of God's family. The prayers are ancient, patterned from the early days of the church and coming from the Holy Scripture. They remind us of salvation history, of Christ's continuing power of His once-and-for-all sacrifice on the cross for the forgiveness of our sins. Everyone has a prayer book from which they participate in the prayers and responses.

"There is a prayer that the priest says to invite the Holy Spirit to come upon the gifts of bread and wine and to change them to be for us the Body and the Blood of our Lord Jesus Christ. This is called the Epiclesis. We believe that after this prayer, the Holy Spirit does come upon these gifts, and that they now represent, for us, the real presence of Christ—His Body and His Blood. After this prayer, we join together and pray the Lord's Prayer.

"The words of institution that Christ used were always included, as were songs like 'Sanctus,' 'Holy, Holy, Holy,' and others. They're not just songs but specific lyrics set to music for a specific occasion.

"The person leading the service, usually called the celebrant, will take the bread, give thanks, and break it. This symbolically shows

Christ's body broken, expressing the shared nature of communion. He will also take the cup and give thanks, showing Christ's body, poured out. After the words of institution, which includes, 'Take, eat: This is my body, which is given for you,' and 'Drink this, all of you: This is my Blood of the new Covenant, which is shed for you and for many for the forgiveness of sins,'[2] he administers both the body and the blood to the people of God. As the bread is given, the celebrant says, 'The Body of Christ, the bread of heaven.'[3] And the person receiving the bread (the communicant) will say, 'Amen.' The celebrant then offers the cup, which the communicant can either take a sip of or dip his bread in the wine (called intinction). As the cup is offered, the celebrant says, 'The Blood of Christ, the cup of salvation.'[4] After the communicant takes the wine, either by sipping or intinction, they would say, 'Amen,' and probably make the sign of the cross, which we do for various reasons.

After everyone has communed, praying together, we thank Him for feeding us with the spiritual food in the Sacrament of His Body and Blood. We also asked Him to send us away in peace, strength, love, and courage to serve Him.

Again, there's an ending to the service that follows this second part called the dismissal. There was already a transition to Dismissal from the last prayer asking Him to send us out. During the Dismissal, there could be a song, another prayer, a recessional, but surely there would be a benediction of sorts. The benediction is a prayer spoken by the celebrant that asks us to be strong and faithful and to go out from this place and share the love of Christ. He makes a sign of the

---

[2]   *Anglican Church in North America: The Book of Common Prayer and Administration of the Sacraments* (Anglican Liturgy Press, 2019), 133. Huntington Beach, CA

[3]   Ibid., 136.

[4]   Ibid.

cross toward the parishioners to bless them, and they usually reply by signing themselves.

"Just before they leave, either the Celebrant or a deacon says the formal dismissal like, "Go in peace to love and serve the Lord." And the people reply, 'Thanks be to God.'"

Father Greene once again apologized for running just a little late. He said that he appreciated all the questions, but that it did take time to answer them. He reminded them that next week would be the last week of the workshops and they would be covering the topic of music in worship. They all shook hands or hugged as they were leaving. Father Greene drove home with a smile on his face, thinking how fortunate he was to have such a lovely group of people to work with.

Music

As the group met for the last week of the workshop, Father Greene reminded the faithful members that this was the last week of the workshop. They had discussed the Christian Calendar, the two parts of the service made up of Word and sacrament, and tonight they would be talking about music.

"Music is used as a tool to aid us in worship, but it is not worship itself. Sometimes we forget that music needs to have a purpose and a function. So we first need to ask, 'What is music used for in worship?' We need to carefully notice that our worship has a flow, meaning, purpose, and direction. The music we use needs to be a partner in that flow, with meaning and purpose as well. We can't just randomly pick a song because we like it. The song selection must meet certain criteria if it's to be selected for use in our services.

"There are churches that use different forms or orders for their services. Some are structured in such a way that uses three hymns.

The next week, they just erase those hymns and replace them with three others. Other churches have their music put into sets that are scheduled throughout the service. These sets could contain as many as five songs. Still other churches have a time of music that may last thirty minutes before they play a few slower songs just before the sermon. Then at the end of the service, there may be another song to close with.

"There are many orders of service for all the different faith traditions. Some churches say they don't have a liturgy, but if they have a service order, and they all do, then they have a liturgy. However, our liturgy has been passed down through the ages and is still followed in all the churches throughout the world that share our faith tradition. The only part of our service that changes from other liturgies of our faith is the music. Each church chooses the psalms, hymns, and spiritual songs that their church sings each week for various services.

"Because this is such a huge subject it will be broken down into these parts: One, the role of music in worship; two, the functions of music in worship; three, the selection of music in worship; and four, the presentation of music in worship. This is really just a skeleton of the many aspects of worship music, but there is only a small amount of time to cover this massive topic.

"The role of music in our services is to facilitate the actions of worship. Music does not work on its own. It has to have a purpose, and in worship, its purpose is to facilitate and not to be a platform for displaying talent, or shall we say, showing off. If it calls attention to itself, as a general rule, then it has been inappropriately used. So music's role in the service is to facilitate. And though its role is to facilitate, it has many functions.

The function of music in the service of worship can take many forms. It can be used to accompany the actions of worship, like prayer, praise, and proclamation. It can be used to accommodate the dialogue of worship, like the responses. It can accomplish a communal ministry of worship. Music can be used for sung praise, sung proclamation, and sung prayer. Some can be with words and sometimes just instrumental according to its accompanying of the action of worship for which it's used."

After answering a few questions concerning the role and function of music in worship, Father Greene returned to his notes and continued, "The selection of music is very important. Every song we sing is part of our own Christian formation. As someone already said, 'We are what we sing.' The songs should not be selected because they are popular. In fact, some leaders often choose songs that are playing on Christian radio stations for their worship services. It is a terribly important job to select songs not because they are popular or because we like them but because they are good for our formation and glorifying to God. Typically, if hymns have survived for hundreds of years, then they are probably safe to choose from. One more point to remember is that singing is also praying, so be careful what the lyrics are.

"Finally, it's very important how the music is presented. Our church building is not built with a choir loft front and center. Has anyone ever wondered why? Of course not, unless you come from a tradition that had a choir loft front and center, you never noticed that was different. The architects of liturgical buildings always made sure that the altar of the Lord was always front and center. Our church is built in a cruciform pattern, which is the shape of a cross. The arms of the cross are called transepts. So the choir sits either in the transepts or in the balcony behind the people. There are rarely any musicians, instrumental or vocal, that are ever seen by the people. You might say that everything musical in our church happens behind the scenes.

"Now this isn't true for other faith traditions. Many years back, it was believed that having musicians that were seen by the people was more appropriate. People wanted to see the musicians. It was a reasonable thought, but the problem was that once the musicians had an audience, more and more people were asking to be a part of the music ministry to be seen. It became more of a production of entertainment than a service of worship."

To wrap everything up, Father Greene summarized the workshop.

"It doesn't matter if we are talking about worship or bake sales, we always represent God the best way we know how. We've talked about the Christian Calendar and why we use it. We've talked about how our worship is basically a fourfold pattern broken into two main parts: Word and Sacrament. We've talked about the role, function, selection, and presentation of music in our worship services and its function. Please remember these things and think about them. If you have questions, please let me know."

And with that, they prayed and then departed for their homes.

Freedom Church, Elder Board Meeting

At 9:00 a.m., the Elder Board arrived at Freedom Church. Pastor Marshall invited them into his office. Their expressions ranged from mad to sad to worried to embarrassed. Penny was right behind them with coffee for everyone.

Claude spoke first. "Pastor Marshall, I know you think you are where the buck stops, but that's not true—"

Pastor Marshall interrupted. "But that's exactly what my contract says. I have it right here."

Claude said, "Put it away. Every one of us here helped draw up that contract before you even came. What it really means is that you are responsible for the spiritual side of things around here, not the financial. We take care of that."

Pastor Marshall thought about that for a quick moment. "That might not be a bad idea." But then he remembered that they were his flock, and he couldn't let them act without thinking. He said, "Guys! I'm not trying to muscle you. I don't think I'm in charge of everything. There's no way I could be. I need the help of everyone. But I was told by the committee that nominated me that I had the last say on everything. I really don't know as much as you all do about finances. My responsibility to God and to you is to make sure you think before you act."

Claude said, "Do you think you are our father? We are twice your age, which means we have twice as much wisdom and experience as you. You need to go work on your sermon and visit the sick folks and leave the church decisions up to us."

Nash Franks spoke up. "Guys, we don't need to get all worked up about this. All we need to do is convince the good pastor here that his talents are better used working on ministry. Plain and simple."

Pastor Marshall couldn't hold back, so he said, "Listen! I didn't surrender to the ministry to be pushed around by church bullies. God called me here to lead. And lead, I will."

Bud Spear said, "Pastor Marshall, please don't get all upset with us. We are just saying, since the Elder Board members tithe 90 percent of what's given to the church, we should probably be the ones having the final say on how things are spent."

Pastor Marshall said, "Bud, I thank you for trying to be calm in all this, but that's simply not how it works. You see, when we give to the Lord's work, be it the offering, missions, or whatever, it is given with no strings attached. Once it's given, you no longer have control of it. However, you are a part of this local community, so you have a say, with your vote, in business meetings."

Everyone was getting a little aggravated. They both had good points. On the one hand, they give a lot of money and should have more of a say. But on the other hand, they are part of a larger group serving God under a godly leader. Nothing is really ours anyway—it all belongs to God. Tensions grew as the silence lingered.

"I've had enough," said Claude. "This is how it's going to be. Pastor Marshall will step aside from financial matters concerning the church. And that's that!"

"And if I refuse?" asked Pastor Marshall.

"Then the offering plate will be pretty empty for a while," said Claude. "So I guess you can make that financial decision, right?"

Claude led the Elder Board out of the office. Pastor Marshall sat in his office rethinking all that had just happened. If he lived by his conviction, he would call a church meeting and put a stop to all this nonsense. But if he did, he would surely be poking the flames of a vicious fire.

There are times in life when decisions are really hard to make. Pastor Marshall knew that things were not going well in his church and that his job was probably in jeopardy. If he stood up against the Elder Board, they would surely withhold their tithes and put the church in financial despair. What was he to do? He knew that God had called him to be a servant—first to God, then to his people. If he allowed them to overstep their authority, then he wouldn't be doing his job. If he allowed them to make decisions without thinking about the consequences to the entire congregation, they were in deep trouble. If he was to just back down, then he was no leader at all. He had to decide if he would allow them to bully him into submission or make a stand even if it cost him his job.

Freedom Church, Called Meeting

Because of the gravity of the situation facing the church, Pastor Marshall called a meeting of the entire church. He had to try his best to unite the church before the chaos ensued. He asked Penny to contact all church members immediately and persuade them all to come to the church tonight at 7:00 p.m. for a very important meeting.

Penny was a very loyal and dedicated secretary, and she jumped right on the task. The church wasn't that large, so by noon, she had contacted everyone by phone, and if she did not get to talk with them, she left a voice message and sent them an email. She talked to approximately 75 percent of the membership and had to hope that the rest would either check their phone messages or email before this evening.

Pastor Marshall canceled all his meetings and appointments for the entire day so he could spend all his available time preparing for the meeting. He consulted his job description, emails with any discussion about his position as senior pastor, his library of books on church politics, and, of course, the Bible on church leadership. By 6:00 p.m., he was exhausted and nervous, but he was prepared to sacrifice all to protect his flock.

By 6:40 p.m., people had begun to gather in the sanctuary. Pastor Marshall was there to greet them at the entrance. Many of those who came were wondering why there was an important meeting. They had been in the meeting where Claude created an incident, but they really weren't sure why they were called to this "important" meeting. Pastor Marshall saw the looks on their faces, and this troubled him deeply. This was his flock, and they were under his care. He had to protect them from the possible tragedy that awaited.

Pastor Marshall called the meeting to order. He said that the minutes from the last meeting would not need to be read because this was a special called meeting and not a regular scheduled meeting. He reminded them of the past church meeting where he adjourned the meeting early because it had gotten out of hand. According to this job description he had been given by the church upon his employment there, he had the authority to end a meeting when he felt it was not in the best interest of the church to continue. After that, he read his job description to verify. He asked if everyone understood, and even asked for a show of hands. Everyone understood—even Claude.

Next, Pastor Marshall went into detail, again, about the meeting with Ted and Alicia Wilson a few weeks prior, in which they presented a list of suggestions that may increase church growth. From there he told them about the meeting with the Elder Board, which he was unavoidably late for, and that they had started without him. By the time he arrived, they had already gone through the list and made decisions without his input. Further, they had not allowed him to have a voice. He continued that the last church meeting they had, there was an attempt to railroad the membership to go in a direction that had no spiritual input or discussion about ramifications that may result in a decision to follow this list. The meeting was rightfully adjourned because of the spirit in which it transpired. However, there was another meeting the very next morning with the Elder Board that proved to be vicious.

After explaining all this to the membership, Pastor Marshall shared with them about the necessity of the church leadership to stay God-focused in their journey. He shared with them from Hebrews 13:17, which states, "Obey your leaders and submit to them, since they keep watch over your souls as those who will give an account, so that they can do this with joy and not with grief, for that would be unprofitable for you."

He told them that since he had been called to the ministry, he had always put God before pleasure and before comfort. He said, "It's not easy for me to make a stand. But for God and for righteousness, I cannot do anything else. Otherwise, I would be counted unworthy to be your pastor."

Claude stood up. Pastor Marshall's blood ran cold. It was as if Satan himself stood up.

Claude said, "Pastor Marshall, that's all well and good. But the truth is, we have the final say. We are the ones who give of our time and talents to keep this church afloat. We ultimately have the final say. And the Elder Board has already told you, we have voted to please God by moving forward to do the items on the list to the glory of God."

Several from the congregation said, "Amen!"

Pastor Marshall would not give up on his people. He pleaded with them to open their eyes to manipulation. He reminded them about the Hebrews whom God had rescued from captivity. He reminded them of how Moses was given the commandments, but they had already fashioned a golden calf to worship because they couldn't wait for God. He pleaded for them to wait, pray, meditate on God's Word before they made any decision that was not directed by the Holy Spirit. He told them how much he loved God and was convicted to help them to stay focused on what makes God happy and not on what might make them happy.

As the meeting continued, there were several questions that seemed to lead to what the people wanted versus what God wanted. Pastor Marshall fielded the questions as best he could, but it seemed that maybe the Elder Board had already made contact with the majority of the congregation before the meeting was called. Again, the question, at least for Pastor Marshall, was whether to submit to the desires of the congregation or stand firm.

The meeting was over. Pastor Marshall retired to his office. He prayed, "God, what am I to do?" He waited for a response, but there was none. Sometimes God wants us to think for ourselves. What is right? What is wrong? These are the question that plague all of us. We have to decide, and make that decision, for every question in our lives. Usually, God will reveal to us what He wants. Sometimes, He wants us to decide. Pastor Marshall felt defeated. What would be the outcome?

Freedom Church, Another Called Meeting

A few days had passed since the called church meeting. Pastor Marshall was preparing his sermon for Sunday service when Penny knocked on his door.

"Come in," said Pastor Marshall.

Penny entered and sat down. She had a worried look on her face.

"What's the matter, Penny?" asked Pastor Marshall.

Penny said, "I just received a call from Claude Nelson. He and the rest of the Elder Board have asked me to calendar a called church meeting for tomorrow night."

Pastor Marshall said, "Well, that can't be good."

"Pastor Marshall," said Penny, "I am so sorry about all this. I know how you are trying to protect the church from making a really bad mistake, but this may really turn bad. The talk at Daulphy's is that a large majority of the church is in favor of making the changes, going in debt, and overstepping you if you don't get on board. I really don't want to see that happen. In fact, all this makes me sick to my stomach."

"Penny, we must always strive to do what's right, no matter the cost," said Pastor Marshall.

Penny left the office and reluctantly scheduled the meeting.

By that afternoon, Pastor Marshall had already received nine phone calls from people wanting to meet with him to talk about the suggestions. He scheduled a couple of meetings for that afternoon and the rest for the next morning. The sermon would have to wait.

That afternoon, he met with Mr. and Mrs. Downey, who were adamant about moving forward with the changes suggested by the Wilsons. They were even going to donate the first ten thousand dollars to the cause. In fact, they had already written the check and earmarked it for the Suggestion List Project, so the money could not be used for anything else.

As they were leaving, they said, "Pastor, I sure hope you get on board with this thing. It's going to be great for our church!"

The next meeting was with a widow named Julie Long. The dear sweet lady lived on a fixed income but was tithed to the church regularly and faithfully. Pastor Marshall began to explain that he was not against some changes being made, but there were some that he felt weren't necessary for the church or for church growth. He just wanted everyone to slow down and think. As he was talking, he could tell that she wasn't paying attention to what he was saying.

When he stopped, she said, "Now, Pastor, I've been a part of church life since I was a child and never lost my faith. I've been in this church since it started, which makes me a charter member. I've given what little I can to the church every week because that's how I believe. I'm old, and I choose to do what I choose to do, and I choose to support the changes that everybody but you want to make. You should want this for us too."

Pastor Marshall was feeling more defeated by the moment. What would it mean if the church moved forward without his approval? If he didn't get fired, would he even want to stay after they ignored his leadership? Either way, it looked as though his days at Freedom Church were numbered.

The next morning, Pastor Marshall had seven more meetings. Each person who came in that morning was all for making the changes and taking on the debt—except one man, Bernie Moffit. Bernie had some odd and unusual ideas about life, especially the spiritual life. He didn't think that you have to be in church every time the church doors were opened. He didn't think you had to take communion, or even be baptized. His views on tithing leaned more toward "Give to the poor and the needy, and God would keep the church doors opened."

Bernie said, "Pastor Marshall, I'm in favor of making the changes, but I'm not in favor of going in debt so deeply that we can't get out. But I'm going to vote that we make the changes anyway, because that's what everyone else wants, and I just don't want to be the black sheep."

Well, thought Pastor Marshall, *I guess that confirms it. The church is going to bypass my leadership and vote to go in depth to make way for church growth.*

He began to pray and ask God for wisdom to know what to do and say in this meeting. He wasn't afraid of losing his job, but he was concerned that the people were making a decision based on personal pride. The idea of right and wrong was not even a thought in their heads, and they would not stop long enough to consider how long it would take to pay off the debt. In his opinion, it was just bad stewardship. Like it or not, the meeting was just a couple hours away.

As the people entered the church for the meeting, Pastor Marshall was there to greet them. Everyone was as friendly as they could be. Pastor Marshall just kept thinking of how this innocent, loving people were about to make a huge mistake. Claude made his entrance with a couple other Elder Board members close behind. Claude saw Pastor Marshall and turned away, as did the other board members who were with him.

Pastor Marshall chased Claude down to shake his hand and welcome him to the meeting.

Claude said, "I don't fraternize with the enemy."

Pastor Marshall said, "Now, Claude, you know I'm not the enemy. I'm just a voice trying to be heard so that all these wonderful people know the truth."

Claude said, "They know the truth. We've met with every one of these people here tonight and explained to them how you don't want us to grow."

"That couldn't be farther from the truth," said Pastor Marshall. "Have you not heard anything I've said? I just wanted you and everyone else to pray and consider whether this project is to give glory God or ourselves. If it is for God, then let's all get on board, but if—"

Claude held up his hand to stop Pastor Marshall from finishing his statement. "That's all just a bunch of words. We want these changes, and the outcome will glorify God. Now let's just see how everyone votes."

The meeting was called to order. Minutes were read and approved as always.

Pastor Marshall said, "This is a called meeting of the church, so there will be no question for old or new business. Claude Nelson from the Elder Board has called this meeting, so I'll invite him now to share with us the reason for the meeting."

Claude made his way to the front of the church. "Everyone here knows me. I've been a member here from the beginning. I'm a tither, a giver, a servant, and I faithfully attend church every Sunday. Even when we go on trips away, we are in a church on Sunday morning. We have had an opportunity come to us through the giving of a list of suggestions. The Elder Board, of which I am a member, has looked this list over and has determined that it would be a good thing for us to join together and complete all items. Our pastor is against it, and has been from the start."

Pastor Marshall said, "That's not true."

Claude said, "Pastor, with all due respect, I'm talking now. You will have your chance to talk when I'm done."

Pastor Marshall sat down, and Claude continued, "The Elder Board has decided that it's time for the church to determine what it wants to do, so we ask for a vote."

As Claude went back to his seat, Pastor Marshall stood up and said, "In error, Claude made the statement that I'm not in favor, which is not at all true. I am in favor of pleasing God. I am in favor of you knowing what it means to take on this kind of debt. I am in favor of you, having prayed and sought wisdom from God, to decide for yourselves what you want to do. I'm sorry I didn't have the opportunity to talk to you all individually before you made up your minds, but I did meet with a few of you yesterday and today, and I was shocked that your minds were already made up due to a visit to you by our Elder Board. Well, though I have tried to lead you, I'm afraid I already know the outcome, but we shall vote anyway."

There was complete silence as Pastor Marshall continued, "Tonight we are voting to either continue with the entire list of suggestions from the list given to us by Ted and Alicia Wilson or table the discussion and wait for the Lord's guidance."

Claude interrupted, "Pastor, are you suggesting that we haven't already sought wisdom from the Lord?"

"No, Claude," said Pastor Marshall. "I'm saying at this point, you can vote 'Yes' to do the entire list as presented, or to vote 'No,' in which case we would table the discussion. If we were to vote 'No' without tabling it, then the 'No' vote would mean we have voted not to do the list at all."

Someone shouted, "That makes sense, let's just vote now."

Pastor Marshall asked, "Do we have a motion?"

Claude said, "I put this in the form of a motion."

"Second?" asked Pastor Marshall.

Bud Spear said, "I second the motion."

Pastor Marshall cleared his voice and said, "All those in favor of doing the entire list of suggestions given to us by Ted and Alicia Wilson, please show by raised hand."

As the hands went up, assigned counters recorded the number of people who voted. After the hands were counted, Pastor Marshall said, "Please lower your hands. All those in favor of tabling the motion to a later date, please raise your hand."

Only one hand went up. It was the hand of Penny, the church secretary. The counters brought their tally to Pastor Marshall to be announced. There were 98 people present for the meeting.

Pastor Marshall announced, "The motion to do the entire list as presented by Ted and Alicia Wilson has passed 97 to 1. Thank you all for representing your church by being here tonight. Let's dismiss with a prayer."

Claude stood up and walked toward the front of the church. He said, "Pastor, before we dismiss, there's just one more thing."

"What's that?" asked Pastor Marshall.

Claude grabbed a microphone and said to the congregation, "Thank you all for standing firm in your convictions. I believe that the majority vote shows that we as a church are strong enough to stand against a corrupt leader."

Jaws dropped on hearing Claude's words.

Pastor Marshall's heart missed a few beats.

"He has tried to lead us astray, but we stood together proving that we no longer need his leadership in our church, and I move that we ask for his resignation."

New Life Church, Special Meeting

Reverend Jane was elated that the church was moving forward with the entire list! She was thinking that their church may grow to be the largest church in the city. And the most wonderful thing about it was that the entire church body was in favor. What could go wrong?

She had already started contacting capital campaign organizations to obtain funding. She was dancing on the clouds, so to speak. She would be featured in newspapers and journal articles around the area as the one who led the congregation to prominence and recognition as the fastest growing and the largest congregation in Faithville! Oh, what an honor!

As she was thinking, there probably needed to be a formal church agreement on what they are doing. So she called a "special meeting" of all church members. She sent out an email inviting all members to a "special meeting" after this week's Sunday morning service. Invitations were sent, and the meeting was set.

At the end of the next Sunday service, Reverend Jane announced that a meeting of the church membership would follow. All those who were not members were dismissed, and all those who were members were invited to remain. After the nonmembers had left, Reverend Jane addressed the congregation.

"Dear friends, we decided at our regular church meeting to move forward with the suggestion list that was provided to us. You have also encouraged me to look for a lending company to secure funds for this project. I have called this meeting to keep you informed of the progress made toward accomplishing this task. I have contacted a number of banks, lending agencies, and private lenders. What I have found is that we must prepare to pay a pretty high percentage rate as well as use our existing property as collateral. Every place I contacted has a high lending rate. Because we are a nonprofit entity, we can get a lower rate, but that rate is still pretty high. You met Jonathan Zahn at our last meeting, and you voted to have his company do our capital campaign. Jonathan has informed me of new rates that have come out, and they are higher than before. We have not signed any contract, so we are not bound by any rates as of yet. I have chosen a new company that would provide us with a capital fundraising campaign team, which seems like the right thing to do since we don't have any financial organizations represented in our church family. So I bring this suggestion to you, the church body, now."

Reverend Jane answered numerous questions concerning the loan, interest rates, payback amounts, etc. The meeting lasted for more than an hour. Everyone was exhausted and hungry. At the end, when questions had subsided, Reverend Jane asked for a vote to approve moving forward with securing T&A Finance as the capital fundraising company at an interest rate of 9.2 percent. Even though that seemed like an extremely high rate, that was the best offer they had received from every contact made.

Reverend Jane explained that the estimate for all funding they would need amounts to a monthly note of $2,737.89 for twenty years, which would be paying back $357,092.67 at that interest rate. If they changed to ten years, the monthly note would be $3,832.82, which would be paying back $159,938.52 at that interest rate. After another lengthy discussion of interest paid back and monthly rates, the congregation was much more concerned about making that monthly note than paying back over twice what they were borrowing.

Reverend Jane asked if someone would like to make a motion.

Bob Taylor stood up and said, "I put in the form of a motion that we use T&A Finance as our capital campaign company at an interest rate of 9.2 percent for twenty years."

Nancy Sullivan said, "I second that motion."

Reverend Jane said, "All those in favor, please show by raised hand."

Almost every hand went up.

Then she said, "All those opposed by like sign."

No hands went up.

She said, "Motion carried."

A hand went up after the vote.

Reverend Jane said, "Yes, what is your question?"

Scott Peterson stood up and asked, "Is there any estimate of when all this is to start?"

Reverend Jane said, "I talked with the team leader, Joe Myers, for the capital campaign, and he said he could meet with us before the end of the month, and after he had secured enough initial partnerships with contributors, we could secure the loan. So my guess is by next month, Lord willing."

Everyone applauded.

Reverend Jane retired to her office and made some tea. She sat back and imagined what it would be like to have double, or even triple, the people they have now. A smile broke out across her face as she was swept away with thoughts of what could happen. She giggled aloud and finished her tea.

Chapter

SEVEN

THE INVESTMENT

Holy Cross Church

During the next few days, Father Greene talked to several lenders about the options for loans. Interest rates were high, but if they took on one project at a time and raised most of the money before they took out a loan, it would be easier and safer. The best rate he found was from T&A Finance.

As the church council met to decide which project should be first, Father Greene suggested that everyone mark five items and prioritize them with numbers 1 through 5. Mrs. Alexander had made priority sheets to make it easier for them. The sheets were already numbered 1 through 5, so all they had to do was jot down their choices.

After a few moments, the sheets had all been turned in to Larry Pritchard.

Larry said, "It looks like the majority chose changing the church colors as their first choice and remodeling the church entrance as their second choice."

Father Greene said, "Okay, then, let's get prices on both those items to see what that will cost."

Edward Reece asked, "Are we thinking of remodeling the outside or the inside of the entrance, or both? If we are talking about the outside, then that would need to be done before we change the colors of the church. Otherwise, we would have to repaint."

"Good thinking," said Father Greene.

Sammy Samuels said, "I have a couple good friends that are in construction. How about I meet with them and get a few suggestions? They may even give us a bid for the work."

"Great idea," said Edward.

Father Greene said, "It looks like we have a plan to move forward. Let's all stay in touch. I'll have Mrs. Alexander create a group email with you all so everyone is on the same page. After a prayer for guidance, wisdom, and peace, they dismissed.

Father Greene thought it best to let someone other than himself take the lead on securing a loan. He wanted to give oversight, but he didn't want to be the one making the decision of which lender to use. He called a few of the council members before Pete Elliot agreed to research the companies.

Father Greene met with Pete and gave him all the research he had done.

Pete said, "Father Greene, it looks like you have already done the research."

Father Greene replied, "Pete, that's just some preliminary research. It looks like we don't take in enough money monthly and our property value is not enough to secure great rates. T&A Finance would offer us the lowest rate, but I don't know anything about the company."

Pete decided he would start by researching the companies to see how they are rated and how long they have been in business. "I'll jump on this right away," said Pete.

That afternoon, Father Greene was thinking about what they could do to raise money. Bake sales are fun, as are carwashes, but they never really bring in much money. He decided to call in the Ladies Auxiliary. Hilda Samuels, Sammy's wife, was the leader. Father Greene called Hilda to see if that was something that the Ladies Auxiliary would be interested in taking on as a project. "Hello, Hilda. This is Father Greene. How are you doing today?" "Just wonderful, Father Greene. And how are you?"

"I'm doing well. I was thinking about enlisting you and the other ladies to brainstorm about what our church family could do to raise money for the new projects," said Father Greene.

Hilda said, "We are always looking for a way to serve the church and the community. What did you have in mind?"

"I was wondering if you and the other ladies could brainstorm ways that our church family could raise money for the new projects we are hoping to take on in the near future?" Father Greene asked.

"The loan rates are high. I thought if we could find ways to offset that by raising some money ourselves, it could save us some money."

Hilda said, "That's a smart move, Father Greene. I'll call a meeting and get right to work on it.

It wasn't long before both Pete and Hilda were ready for a meeting. A meeting was set up for Hilda first. When Hilda arrived, Mrs. Alexander had made coffee and carrot cake.

As they finished their cake, Father Greene asked, "So what wonderful ideas did the Ladies Auxiliary come up with?"

He could tell by Hilda's chipper mood that she was anxious to share.

Hilda began, "We have come up with several ideas, and allow me to say, we are so excited! This will be good not only for finances but also for exposure."

Father Greene asked, "What do you mean by exposure?"

Hilda continued, "Well, when we were discussing ideas, we realized that we will be connecting with people all over town, so people will know that Holy Cross Church is out there doing something."

"Ah, I see. Please continue."

"There are basically two ideas that we all agreed were the best. First, we could sell tickets to a lunch of spaghetti, salad, a roll, and a drink. We could have Eric Dooley get all the men of the church to go to the business owners and have them purchase tickets for their workforce. That would help the employees see how much the business owners care about their workers. The Ladies Auxiliary can do the preparing, and the men and the youth that can drive could make the deliveries."

Father Greene said, "That's brilliant! What was the second idea?"

Hilda said, "A commitment card. We ask all the parish members to pray for an amount they could commit to give, over and above their tithe, to help us achieve our goals. The cards are returned with an amount they can give, and it's signed. Each month, we send them a reminder and let them know if they are up to date with their giving commitment."

Father Greene was pleased. "Thank you, Hilda, for all your work on this. Let's move forward."

Pete showed up the next morning for his meeting with Father Greene. He too looked pleased with his findings. As usual, Mrs. Alexander had brought coffee and a treat.

"Father Brown," said Pete, "I've done a lot of research, and you were right—T&A Finance can offer us a better rate. I did the best I could in trying to get background info. There's a little bit of info on the web, but not much. The good thing is, I haven't seen anything bad about them."

"Well, that's good news," said Father Greene.

Pete continued, "So they said we could sign papers and have the loan by the end of the week."

Father Greene said, "But we really don't know how much we need for the first two projects."

Mrs. Alexander knocked on the door. "Yes, come in," said Father Greene.

Mrs. Alexander said, "I hate to interrupt your meeting, but Sammy Samuels is on the phone and has a message for you."

Father Greene picked up the phone and spoke to Sammy.

After a brief conversation with Sammy, he hung up the phone. Father Greene turned to Pete and said, "Sammy has spoken with a couple contractors about the project. He said it looks like we will need about fifteen thousand dollars to complete. He said the Ladies Auxiliary is estimating that they could possibly bring in two thousand dollars with their lunch idea. We have maybe five thousand dollars in our building fund that could be used, but that would leave us short if there are any maintenance issues we would need to attend to. So we need to see how the commitment card idea that the Ladies Auxiliary works out."

Pete said, "If the parish could commit to five thousand dollars, we wouldn't have to drain the building fund, and we would be at the halfway mark," Father Greene said, "I don't see why we couldn't move forward with this. To be safe, maybe we should get a loan for ten thousand dollars if we can afford the monthly note. Any leftover could be used for the next project."

The regular church meeting was coming up, and the commitment card idea had been written in such a way as to not intimidate the people or put pressure on them to give more than they should.

Father Greene was always careful to include and encourage everyone, but never to press them to do anything. As the meeting day approached, Father Greene was drawn to the sanctuary several times to pray. As he prayed, he looked around at the altar, the pews, the pulpit, the stained glass, the figurines, crosses, and the rest of the fixtures that helped him to focus on God. As he prayed for wisdom, it was revealed to him that God is the Creator of all that is. Of course, he already knew that, but sometimes God continues to reveal Himself. As he ended his prayer time, he felt a sense of peace cover him and a smile of understanding stretched across his face.

As the people gathered for the meeting, Father Greene skimmed over his notes one last time. As he called the people together to begin, a passage of scripture popped into his mind. He said, "Let us consider the first part of verse 10 from Psalm 46. It reads, 'Be still and know that I am God.'"

Everyone was silent for a long moment. Father Greene continued, "Let us pray. Father in heaven, you are the source of life and the giver of all things. We your people humbly come before you asking for your guidance in the decisions we make, because we truly want to please you in everything we do. Grant us your grace as we seek you in all we do. Amen."

As always, the meeting was called to order, and the minutes from the last meeting were read and approved. Then came a question for any old business. There was none. Then a question for any new business.

Father Greene said, "This is not new business, just a continuation of the business at hand. We have been gathering information about costs, loans, and a couple of ideas about how we can raise money to offset the loan. First, I would like to ask Sammy Samuels to come share his findings on contractors to do the work."

Sammy came forward and shared the information he had received about the cost and the time it would take to complete the upgrade of the entrance and painting the entire church. He also made a recommendation to go with a company called Tallis Construction.

When he finished, Father Greene said, "Now I would like to ask Pete Elliot to come and share with us what he was able to discover about financing. Pete came and shared his findings and his recommendation that they go with T&A Finance.

"I know we are all concerned about how this project will impact our finances. Well, any construction these days is costly. The items from the list that we have chosen to undertake is not for the purpose of church growth. These items need our attention already. I think it's important for us to remember that scripture teaches us to be wise and 'count the cost' before we jump into anything, and we have. I have asked the Women's Auxiliary to brainstorm and come up with some ideas on how we as a congregation might get involved. I've asked Hilda Samuels to come to share with us those ideas.

Hilda came to the front of the sanctuary with a big grin on her face. She said, "Hi, everybody! I'm excited to share with you a couple ideas that the Ladies Auxiliary came up with. I know you're thinking of a bake sale, but it's not. Instead, we are thinking a lunch delivery."

Hilda explained to the people how it would work. Of course, there were questions and suggestions, but Hilda fielded them all. Then she added, "We also suggest that the entire church participate in a commitment card campaign. This way, even those who can't participate in any other way can participate financially. I'll let Father Greene explain how this will work."

As Hilda returned to her seat, Father Greene said, "I don't think we've ever had a commitment card campaign at this parish before. I think it's a good idea, but I don't want you to be afraid. This is not a public commitment. It's all private—no one knows if you are committing or not, and if you are, no one knows how much. We will send you a commitment card to be filled out and turned in no later than the end of the week. We ask you to pray on what you can commit every month for the next year. This does not include your tithes. As you know, your tithes are what keeps the church functioning. This commitment will be for an amount over and above your normal giving. You should know that when you commit a certain amount, we are counting on you to stay true for a full year, and we will be sending a quarterly statement of your contributions. Together we can keep the church functioning as normal, raise money to offset the loan, and get this project completed."

There were questions about the commitment card campaign, of course. But Father Greene answered them all until everyone seemed at peace. Then he asked, "Do I hear a motion that we move forward with the upgrading of the entrance and painting the church building, secure a loan for the work, and offset the loan with a lunch delivery and commitment card campaign?"

Larry Pritchard stood up and said, "With joy in my heart, I put in the form of a motion what Father Greene just said."

"Do I have a second?" asked Father Greene.

Tim Sullivan said, "I second."

Father Greene said, "All in favor by a show of hands."

Nearly every hand went up. Then Father Greene said, "Any opposed by like sign."

There were three that raised their hands.

Father Greene said, "Motion carried."

David Marks was one of the parishioners that voted no. He stood and said, "Father Greene, I voted 'No' to these projects. I want you all to understand that I have my reasons for voting 'No,' but I am part of this church. So if it would be okay with everyone, could we have another vote?"

Father Greene was moved to tears and said, "Of course, David. Everyone in favor of the motion just made, please raise your hands."

Everyone raised their hands. David Marks stood with hand raised high and a big smile on his face, and so did the other two that had voted 'No.'

Father Greene said, "All those opposed by like sign."

No one raised their hand. "Motion carried by 100 percent of the parish!" shouted Father Greene. The church erupted in applause and cheer.

Freedom Church

It was a sad morning for Pastor Marshall as he made his way to the office. He felt lonely and very much unloved. It wasn't fair that he loved his church and cared so much for them and not a soul cared for him.

As he made his way to his office, Penny was right behind him with fresh coffee.

"Pastor Marshall, I'm so sorry that you are having to endure this. I just feel so bad for you. I know the church loves and respects you—they're just letting their hearts be led by Claude and his gang."

"Gang, you say?" asked Pastor Marshall, and they both laughed. "Thank you for lightening the mood," he said.

As Penny was leaving Pastor Marshall's office, he felt a darkness enter the room. He remembered that this must be what Jesus felt many times in His ministry, especially when the Romans came to arrest Him and His disciples fled. Then Peter denied he knew Him. How that must have crushed Jesus.

Pastor Marshall began to tremble and sob. As he sobbed, he prayed, *Lord, I don't know your will. I don't know what you want me to do, and I feel all alone.*

He sat in silence for what must have been an hour when suddenly, he heard footsteps, and the door swung open. It was Claude and his gang.

About that time, Penny followed them in and said, "I'm sorry, Pastor. They just came in without asking."

"It's okay, Penny. Hi guys! Would you like some coffee?"

Claude said, "No."

Henry Newgent said, "Yes, please." And Claude just frowned at him.

"Penny, would you please get Henry a cup of coffee."

Penny left and closed the door behind her.

"What can I do for you, fellows?" asked Pastor Marshall.

Claude spoke first. "We want your resignation."

Pastor Marshall asked, "Can you tell me why?"

Claude said, "You have not been a strong leader. The whole time you've been here, you have thought only about yourself. You don't do anything but prepare sermons and visit Penny all day. You do funerals, but that's in your contract. Worst of all, you run around thinking we are all supposed to follow your thoughts and opinions, when you're only half our age. You don't know what we know about life and living. Sure, you've been to school and think you know everything there is to know about the Bible, but we've been reading the Bible much longer than you have, and we know a lot more about life."

Penny came back in and handed Henry a cup of coffee. She asked, "Pastor Marshall, would you like me to stay and take notes?"

"No, thank you, Penny. That will be all."

Then Pastor Marshall looked around the room and asked, "Gentlemen, do you all agree with what Claude just stated?"

There was some mumbling that sounded like, *Well ...* and *I guess so.*

Pastor Marshall stood up and asked, "Gentlemen, do you agree or not?"

They all reluctantly said, "Yes."

Claude said, "There, it's unanimous. And don't think we don't know about what you and Penny do behind closed doors."

Pastor Marshall was infuriated.

"That's a bald-faced lie!" he shouted.

Claude just smiled and said, "See there, guys, I told you he was guilty."

Pastor Marshall hung his head. He had been defeated. If he decided to stay and fight, he would just bruise the church. Even though he loved them enough to fight for them, he also loved them enough to keep them from having to face an inter-church battle like this. And, oh, how demoralizing that would be for Penny. Even though nothing romantic had gone on between them, he couldn't put Penny through that.

Then he suddenly remembered Jesus telling His disciples that if they weren't received and their words not heard, then when they depart, they should "shake the dust of your feet."

It was as if God had spoken to him and answered his prayer.

"Okay, gentlemen. You win. What are your expectations of my resignation?" asked Pastor Marshall.

"We expect you to sign the loan agreement with T&A Finance today. Then pack your bags and vacate this office by tomorrow. If so, we will give you three months' severance pay and keep our mouths shut about you and Penny," said Claude.

Pastor Marshall looked into the eyes of every man in the room and said, "You already know there is nothing going on, but I want you to hear it from my lips. There is nothing going on between me and Penny. And as far as signing for the loan, I just can't do that."

Claude threatened, "Then there will be hell to pay. So would you like to reconsider?"

Pastor Marshall thought for a moment and said, "If I sign for a loan and then leave, the church will think I don't love them. Surely you will allow me to explain to them what is happening."

Claude said, "You write your resignation. I will read it and decide if we approve. If so, we will read it. If we don't, you will rewrite it until we do."

Then he led the men out of the office.

Pastor Marshall was at his lowest. He had been despised and rejected. He called for Penny, but she was already entering his office to check on him.

"What happened?" she asked.

Pastor Marshall said, "You had better sit down."

As he told Penny what happened in the meeting, both of them started sobbing.

Penny said, "I will resign so you can stay."

Pastor Marshall said, "It wouldn't change a thing. They want me out of here, and really, there is nothing I can do about it. What concerns me is signing the contract with the loan company. The people will think I left them with a debt, intentionally."

By noon a messenger delivered the contract from T&A Finance. Claude had made sure it arrived by then. Pastor Marshall looked over the contract and decided, for the sake of the church, he would sign it. But he would have to word his resignation in such a way that the people all knew it wasn't by choice. He wrote his resignation and included a sentence that said, "I love you all so much and pray that my signing of the loan contract with T&A Finance doesn't prove to be a bad idea."

He sent the resignation to Claude by email. Within five minutes, Claude had replied that it was acceptable. Pastor Marshall started packing his office, as he relived his memories of serving that congregation.

The next few days were miserable for Pastor Marshall. He was at the lowest point in his life. Sad, lonely, and fearful of the future, he sat in his house and prayed, *Lord, I have failed you. You gave me a flock to watch, and I totally let them down. What will become of me? Where should I go and what should I do? Lord, have mercy on me and please watch over your flock.*

Then he sobbed.

Claude, on the other hand, was very happy. He was in control again and would lead his church to an exciting future. The money for the loan would be available in a couple of days, and he was already looking down at the list again to see what should be done first.

"Ah," he said, "I think we will start with the landscaping."

He called the Elder Board together to get started.

"Gentlemen," Claude began, "let's mark the highest priorities on this list and assign everyone a task. I suggest we start with the landscaping. Henry, I think you should head that one up. Call around and see which company can tackle it with the lowest cost to us. The more we can save, the more we can do."

Henry said, "You got it."

Bud Spear said, "I think we should hire some musicians that can play guitars and drums. That seems to be what attracts younger people. I would be glad to take that on and get prices on the equipment needed."

Claude said, "Excellent, Bud. Get to it."

By the end of the meeting, everyone was assigned at least some part of the nine items on the list they had chosen as highest priority. There was joy and excitement in their hearts as they set out to accomplish what they felt was a leading from God.

New Life Church

The day finally came to meet with the capital campaign team leader, Joe Myers. He drove up in an Audi sports car. He was a polished man, clean cut and well spoken. He wore expensive clothes and a gold watch. You could tell he represented wealth, style, and class.

As the people gathered for the meeting, Reverend Jane visited with Joe. "Shouldn't you be greeting the people and getting to know them?" she asked.

Joe said, "I make it a point not to get personally involved with the people. This is business, not a social gathering."

Reverend Jane was shocked. So she moved around the room and visited with those who were gathering. Everyone seemed to be excited.

When it was time for the meeting, Reverend Jane took her position in the front of the room.

"Everyone, let's take our seats," said Reverend Jane. "Tonight, as promised, we have with us the team leader for the capital campaign—Joe Myers. So please listen to everything he has to say and we can ask questions at the end. Joe, please come up and share with us."

Joe came to the front and introduced himself as a financial success. He said even as a little boy, he knew he wanted to do something great with his life, and he did. He said he had a way with numbers and through belief in himself and by taking risks, he has become financially wealthy. He shared with them how they too could be successful and make this church grow, by having faith, of course, but also by stepping out and taking risks.

By the time he had finished, everyone was full of faith and ready to risk it all for church growth. He asked if there were any questions, and there were a few, but his introductory comments were well thought out and well worded, so there wasn't much left explained. They simply had to follow his leadership, work hard, and give a lot of their finances.

Before the meeting ended, he handed out commitment cards. It asked for each family to commit to give 15 percent of their monthly income, over and above their regular offering to the church, toward this campaign. If they couldn't commit to giving 15 percent, they could sell some property, vehicles, boats, and such to help compensate.

"Bottom line, we've got to get your support to make this work, and that can only happen if everyone does their part and gives."

Then Joe said, "I need those cards signed with monthly amounts or total amounts turned in before you leave. Right now, you are ready to make that decision. I have found that when people are ready to do something great, they often lose sight of what is important if they take too long to decide. Take five minutes to fill them out, then get those cards to the end of your row where we can collect them.

Reverend Jane wasn't happy with how this was handled, though she knew that if this was going to happen, everyone would have to give all they could. She walked back up to the front and began to encourage her people.

"Listen, everyone. I know it's hard, with the economy like it is, to be able to let go of hard-earned money, but let me encourage you to look at this as investing in the kingdom. There is so much we can do for the sake of our Lord and Savior, Jesus Christ, by improving this place. This is maybe a once-in-a-lifetime opportunity. Please pray and dig deep into your soul, and into your pockets, and let's make this happen for Jesus!"

As the cards were passed to the end of the row and collected, she was fearful of what they might contain. There were about 125 people present, which represented about 75 families, and there were about that many cards that came in. As Joe and Reverend Jane started tallying the results, she was amazed at what these people were offering. Each family had agreed to the 15 percent above their tithe, and several even added amounts for the items they would sell.

The people didn't go home. They were waiting for the results. The church treasurer, along with Joe and Reverend Jane, added up the results as fast as they could. In about fifteen minutes, they had the numbers.

Reverend Jane said, "Friends, we have a monthly giving total of $750. Some people are selling land, and they really don't know what they can get for it, or even if it will sell. But I want to thank you for being generous tonight. God bless you all, and have a wonderful evening. You're dismissed."

Joe said, "We can move forward with the loan now that there is some confidence that the money will be coming in to pay the monthly note."

Reverend Jane was smiling now.

It looks like it's really going to happen.

"Thank you, Joe," she said. "When can we get started with our projects?"

Joe said, "I just need to get some paperwork finished for this loan and send a wire transfer to your bank. You should have your funds by tomorrow afternoon."

Chapter

EIGHT

THE DISCOVERY

Several months have passed. Holy Cross Church finished their upgrades of the entrance and the painting of the church, and it looked amazing! All the people were excited and busy with the new projects on the list. They had been able to raise enough money to offset their loan amount and comfortably make the payments without dipping into their general fund or disrupting their maintenance account. Things were looking good, and their church attendance was actually increasing. Some past members were regained, and new members were gained.

Freedom Church had made many changes as well. They had completely landscaped their church grounds and added a playground section for the kids. In addition, they had repainted the church with new colors that attracted the attention of many newcomers. Their service now included drums, guitars, synthesizers, and lights. They were totally high tech with their audio and video presentations. They still didn't have a senior pastor, but their church attendance was growing by leaps and bounds because of all the exciting changes that were being made.

New Life Church was also experiencing growth from the changes they had made to their facilities, service, and marketing methods. Reverend Jane was so excited! They had actually doubled in size in just a few months of the positive changes they had made. She had been interviewed by several social media groups and magazines to see what insights she might have for other church leaders concerning church growth. All seemed to be going so well.

During one interview, Reverend Jane was asked what tips she should give other church leaders about church growth in relation to her recent success.

She replied, "You just need to trust that God will lead you. Just pray and allow God to speak to you and direct you in the direction you need to go. Do not be afraid. Take a risk and just trust God's leadership."

Reverend Jane was living the life! She was at the mountaintop enjoying the fruits of her labor. She could not have been happier if she had won several million dollars playing the lottery.

But then reality struck.

The interviewer asked Reverend Jane a question she wasn't prepared for. The interviewer was Maddie Sparks from WKIG Radio in Faithville, Georgia.

Maddie asked, "Reverend Jane, can you comment about the other church closings?"

Reverend Jane said, "Excuse me? I'm not aware of what you're asking."

Maddie asked, "Are you not aware that since your church attendance has increased, other churches in the areas have been experiencing a decrease in attendance?"

Reverend Jane said, "No, I'm sorry, I am not aware."

Maddie said, "Over the last three months, six area churches have been forced to close their doors and declare bankruptcy due to decreased attendance and giving."

Reverend Jane was shocked. She did not know. Her head began to spin. She excused herself from the interview.

She returned to her office and started researching the internet to see what was going on. There were twelve other churches in the city besides New Life, Freedom Church, and Holy Cross. She found that exactly half of those churches had lost members over the past few months and now were unable to continue because of lack of funds.

Oh my! thought Reverend Jane. *This is terrible! Our increase has caused others a decrease. This is not good.*

She immediately called Father Greene.

Mrs. Alexander answered. "Good afternoon, this is Holy Cross Church, how may I help you?"

Reverend Jane said, "Hi there, Mrs. Alexander, this is Reverend Jane from New Life Church, may I please speak to Father Greene?"

Mrs. Alexander said, "I'm so sorry, Reverend Jane, but Father Greene is making a hospital visit. May I take a note?"

Reverend Jane said, "Yes. Would you please ask Father Greene to call me as soon as possible? It is of utmost importance."

Mrs. Alexander said, "Of course I will. I will try to reach him on his cell phone and have him call you as soon as he can."

Within ten minutes, Father Greene called Reverend Jane.

"Hello, Reverend Jane, this is Father Greene."

"Thank you for returning my call," said Reverend Jane.

"I'm terribly disturbed about the news I just received."

"What's that?" asked Father Greene.

"Several churches in our city have closed due to lack of attendance and funds. I'm afraid this might be due to our increase in attendance and funds at New Life church."

Father Greene said, "Now, Reverend Jane, you can't blame yourself for the increase of church membership. People will do what people will do. You are not responsible for that if you offer them an opportunity to worship with you."

Reverend Jane responded, "But, Father Greene, this is not what we intended when we made changes to our church. We wanted to grow, but not at the expense of other churches being unable to function."

They talked for a few minutes and decided to research the issues and stay in touch.

Over the next week, they both called the other churches in the city to check on them. They found that church attendance and giving had fallen drastically. They found that Freedom Church had increased attendance by 90 percent. Most of the churches in the city had lost members to Freedom Church. Father Greene and Reverend Jane decided to pay a visit to Freedom church on Monday to see what was going on there.

On Monday, Father Greene and Reverend Jane met in the parking lot of Freedom Church. They spoke briefly about their intention and then entered the church office.

Penny greeted them with a big smile and asked how she might assist them. They asked if they could speak with Pastor Marshall.

Penny's expression turned to one of extreme sadness, and she said, "I'm sorry, but Pastor Marshall is no longer with us."

Reverend Jane asked, "Well, who is the new pastor?"

Penny said, "We actually don't have a pastor right now."

Father Greene and Reverend Jane just looked at each other.

Father Greene asked, "Then who is in charge?"

Penny said, "That would be Claude Nelson, the head of the Elder Board."

Father Greene could tell that Penny wasn't too happy about that. He and Reverend Jane left.

Back at his office, Father Greene called Claude Nelson. The Elder Board didn't answer, so he left a message.

"Hello, Mr. Nelson, this is Father Greene from Holy Cross Church. Could you please return my call as soon as you are available?"

Father Greene left his number and hung up. He wondered what happened to Pastor Marshall.

After a few calls, Father Greene discovered that Pastor Marshall was working at a sporting goods store. *How strange*, he thought. He immediately paid the pastor a visit at Hayney's Sporting Goods, where he was working in the fishing supplies section. Father Greene approached him from behind and asked if he could be directed to the retired pastor's section.

Pastor Marshall turned around and greeted Father Greene with a hug and a tearful smile.

"Father Greene! How are you?" asked Pastor Marshall.

"I'm good, Pastor Marshall. But how are you?"

Pastor Marshall began to tear up. "I'm not good, Father Greene. I'm a failure, and I really don't know why."

Father Greene said, "Pastor Marshall, you're not a failure—this I know. Please tell me what happened over the past few months at your church."

"I get off work in about forty-five minutes. Can we meet at Dauphy's and talk?"

Father Greene said, "I will be there waiting on you, my friend."

They met at Dauphy's Diner just after five that afternoon. Pastor Marshall told Father Greene everything that had transpired over the past few months, which led to his resignation and his being employed at Hayney's. Father Greene expressed his deep sadness over his friend's situation. He also told Pastor Marshall that he knew that he was a righteous man, representing God in all that has been done, trying his best to protect and guard his congregation from harm.

Father Greene went on to tell Pastor Marshall what was going on with regarding growth among the churches that had made improvements from the list given by the Wilsons. He also told him about the closing of six churches in their community due to lost members and finances from those lost members.

"It's just not right," said Father Greene. "We must rectify this matter."

He suggested that there should be a meeting of the leadership of Holy Cross, New Life, and Freedom Church to come up with a solution to this problem. God's church, which includes all denominations across this city, should be working together as the one body of Christ, not independent churches working on their own.

Chapter

NINE

THE SHOCK

It was the end of October, and the fall weather in Faithville was beautiful. Thanksgiving would soon be upon them. Father Greene thought it would be wonderful if the entire town came together to celebrate Thanksgiving as a community. They could worship together and have activities in the town square. There could be food, festivities, music, and maybe a hayride. The whole town could be together—undivided.

Father Greene asked Mrs. Alexander to contact all the local church leadership to meet about a community Thanksgiving celebration. They would need to move pretty quickly to get everything together. Mrs. Alexander suggested Tuesday evening at six. Father Greene agreed. Mrs. Alexander was already making a list.

By lunchtime, Mrs. Alexander had contacted all the churches, and they were contacting their leadership groups. Once again, there was excitement in the air. That afternoon all the churches had responded positively that their leadership teams would all be there, except for the churches that had closed. There was, however, some tension about where the meeting would take place. It was assumed they would meet at Holy Cross, since Father Greene had the idea, but there was some grumbling about meeting at any church, assuming they were trying get more exposure to the town.

Father Greene made a call to the mayor and asked if it would be possible to have their meeting in the town hall. The mayor liked the idea of a communitywide Thanksgiving celebration and offered the town hall as the meeting place and asked if he could be part of the celebration as well.

"Mayor Townsend, that would be marvelous!" said Father Greene. Then Father Greene explained to the mayor what had been going on and his idea to bring the town together as one body instead of a divided body so that the town might live in harmony. The mayor was elated!

Mrs. Alexander contacted all the churches and asked if the town hall was acceptable to everyone, and it was. So the meeting was scheduled. Father Greene was hopeful that this meeting to plan a celebration together would bring everyone closer and maybe start to tear down the denominational barriers that have plagued this town for years.

Tuesday evening was suddenly here. There were more than one hundred people representing the leadership of all the churches. They were all fairly cheery and smiling. Father Greene was at the entrance welcoming people as they entered.

What a lovely group of people, he thought.

As 6:00 p.m. approached, Father Greene made his way to the front, welcomed everyone, and asked them to please be seated.

Father Greene began, "In all the years I've been in Faithville, we've never had a communitywide Thanksgiving celebration, so I thought we should all come together to discuss that possibility."

A hand went up.

"Yes, is there a question?"

A voice from the crowd asked, "Who put Holy Cross Church in charge?"

Father Greene was shocked! He responded, "Holy Cross is not in charge, and I'm not in charge. My friends, this is not a competition. I simply had an idea I wanted to share with you all to get a consensus of whether or not it is a good idea."

Another hand went up.

"Yes," said Father Greene.

"Shouldn't we decide what church should be in charge?"

Again, Father Greene was shocked! These people had been subjected to division for so long they had no idea what unity looked like.

Mayor Townsend stepped up and apologized to Father Greene. He turned to the people and said, "Please everyone, try to understand what is going on here. This is not a competition for recognition of your church. Father Greene is simply trying to share an idea with you about doing something together. Everyone knows that our town has been divided for years. It's really not about politics, which is usually the culprit, but this town has divided itself over denominational differences. Isn't it apparent to you all that God is our example of love, yet we don't love our neighbors? I've been your mayor for the past eight years, and I have seen how you treat your neighbors in the stores, on the streets, and in meetings that we have had previously. This is not something new. I've lived here the majority of my life, and it's always been this way. Most recently, you have all been competing over church membership—so much that several churches have closed. Is this what you want?"

There was mumbling and chatter among the people. Father Greene thanked the mayor and moved back to the front. "Dear people, change is a hard thing. The older we get, the harder it is to change—I can attest to that. But we are the people of God, are we not? The greatest commandments are these two: Love God above all, and love your neighbor as yourself. Your neighbor is actually everyone around you. They are the people on the street, in the stores, and in the meetings you attend. I would say even the stranger you might meet tomorrow. Your neighbors may be Baptist, Methodist, Pentecostal, or any other tradition, but they are all your neighbors. Yes, even your brothers and sisters in Christ Jesus."

It got very quiet.

Father Greene continued, "Aren't you all ready to stop looking down on people who believe differently than you?"

A man stood up and said, "Father Greene, my name is Ed Fletcher. I've spent my entire adulthood studying the scriptures for truth, and I've determined that the Bible is inerrant and infallible. What it says is true. So if your church doesn't believe the premillennial dispensationalist view, then they aren't true Christians, and we aren't to associate with un-Christian people. That's Matthew 25:31." Lots of people started agreeing with Ed and they got louder.

Father Greene couldn't believe what he was hearing. He held up his hands to quiet the crowd. He said, "Please, people, listen." He picked up his Bible and held it to his ear. "Do you hear that?"

Everyone was quiet.

"It's not making a sound. The Bible, my friends, does not say anything."

The people were shocked! Some booed, some laughed, one person even screamed, "Heresy!"

Again, Father Greene held up his hands to quiet them. "Please understand. The Bible is composed of words. Words are symbols for meaning, and from biblical times, those meanings were based on the culture of the people. You can't just read words and take them literally. You have to figure out *who* they were written for and *why* they were written. In other words, you have to interpret the meaning. Otherwise, no one would call me Father Greene if they took Matthew 23:9 literally. It says, 'And call no man father upon the earth: for One is your father, which is in heaven.' And do the gospels not teach that we are not to judge, or we will be judged? How can you possibly say someone is not a Christian? How can you be their judge? How do you know if they are following Christ to the best of their ability?"

Once again, the mayor intervened. "People, we really need to focus on whether or not we want to move forward with the idea of celebrating Thanksgiving together and not resolving all our issues in this short time together."

Father Greene apologized to Mayor Townsend and to the people. "May I suggest that we all think for a few minutes about the possibility of coming together as a community to prepare a festival of sorts in the town square on Thanksgiving Day. There can be food and festivities for adults and children alike. Afterwards, we can meet together and worship as one body of Christ and give thanks to Him who created us, this town, our nation, and the world and all that lives in it."

A hand went up. Father Greene was excited that finally someone was going to recognize this as a great idea and ask that they move forward.

However, the voice asked, "And which pastor will lead that service?"

Again, Father Greene was shocked! Another hand went up, "And whose church will we worship in?"

Father Greene said, "Our division is causing nothing but controversy. May I suggest we determine if we as a community want to join together and try to overcome diversity with unity or if we are all completely satisfied with the way things are now. We can worship under a tree for all it matters. The idea is that we join together."

Then Father Greene turned to the mayor and asked, "Mayor Townsend, would it be all right to use the town hall for a worship space?"

The mayor said, "I don't see why not. It's certainly large enough. I will go ahead and say yes, but I will meet with the city commissioners to make sure there are no problems."

Father Greene said, "We have pending permission to use the town hall as our worship space. I will meet with all the pastors of the churches to plan a service of worship, and all the pastors will lead together."

The crowd seemed pleased.

Committees were formed, tasks were distributed to all the church leadership, the mayor later gave full approval to use the town hall as the worship space, and all seemed well. Father Greene and all the pastors in charge of a church were invited to help plan. Father Greene also included Pastor Marshall even though we wasn't currently serving a church.

Chapter

TEN

THE INITIAL PLANNING

Including Pastor Marshall and Father Greene, there were sixteen pastors that met on Thursday afternoon to start planning the worship service for the communitywide Thanksgiving gathering. Everyone was elated that the idea had been presented because they were quite tired of hearing all the bad talk in town. Reverend Jane was acting as the spokesperson for the other church leaders because she actually knew them all.

As they began discussing the worship service, it became apparent that few, if any, of the pastors knew anything about worship. They only really knew that the sermon, in their opinion, was the centerpiece of worship. Music was the introduction to the sermon.

Father Greene was a bit distraught. He stood up and said, "Fellow pastors, the worship of God is our ministry to God. We were created to worship Him. That is our function in this world and the world to come. This is what we teach our people."

After that, pretty much all the pastors became reliant on Father Greene to give them guidance in preparing the service. Father Greene accepted the charge and began to suggest that the worship of God was a prayer or dialogue with God. Everyone seemed to be receptive, so he continued.

"God longs for us to commune with Him. We do so by inviting Him to join us as we worship Him. We read His Word, we thank Him by breaking bread and drinking wine (which we are commanded to do—in remembrance), and we dismiss to spread His love throughout our community and to the world."

Everyone agreed that Father Greene should lead them in planning the worship service.

After hours of discussion, everyone agreed to this "new" idea of a worship service that kept God as the central figure. Not only was it God centered, it was Trinitarian. God, the Father, God the Son and, God the Holy Spirit were all included—Trinitarian. There were questions from the pastors.

"Father Greene," asked one pastor, "are you suggesting that in our services of worship we should always include the Trinity and not just Jesus?"

"Yes, I am," replied Father Greene. "Our worship is not only to Jesus but to the One God—Father, Son, and Holy Spirit. They are three-in-one. God manifested Himself in Christ Jesus. God and the Spirit are one with Christ Jesus as testified by the Creeds. They are one as the Trinity. So yes, they should be recognized as one.

Another question came from the group: "Father Greene, please explain to us the idea of sacramentalism. I have heard about it, and I am intrigued."

Father Greene said, "Sacramentalism is about the outward and visible sign of an inward and spiritual grace. That really means that we see something that is beyond our ability to comprehend. The elements that are consecrated—the bread and the wine—are turned into something that is no longer the same. The bread becomes His body, and the wine becomes His blood. It is really not a scientific transformation, but it is a spiritual transformation for us as believers. The bread is no longer bread, it is now His body. And the wine is no longer wine, it is now His blood. It's called, we believe, His presence, or real presence. It becomes, for us, the real body and blood of Christ. So we partake of His body and His blood in true communion."

Father Greene continued, "I am aware that many of you see communion as only a 'remembrance' of Christ's suffering and death. That is all right. We, as a group, trying to restore unity among the churches, just need to agree which approach to take."

The pastors had never heard this teaching before, and they were intrigued. Another hand went up.

"Father Greene, this all seems extremely complicated," said Pastor Larry Jenkins. "Can't we just sing some songs and preach? I mean no disrespect, but that's what pretty much all of our churches do. We don't have an order or a liturgy. We just meet to praise God through song and hear His word preached."

Others agreed. Pastor Marshall finally stood and said, "I've known Father Greene for many years, and I have visited his worship services in the past. There's one thing I know—they are always reverent. They have a purpose for everything they do. And while I don't understand everything that goes on, I think this might be a really good time for us to venture out of our comfort zones and allow Father Greene to teach us some things about how their services are constructed. We might all learn something."

Several pastors agreed.

Father Greene said, "Well then, if you would allow me, I can walk you through the stages, and maybe we could agree on what might be beneficial for an ecumenical service."

Another hand went up. "Father Greene, I'm Claude Nelson from Freedom Church. I'm sure I'm not the only one here who doesn't understand the terms you're using. Could you please explain what these terms mean when you use them?"

"Certainly," said Father Greene. "And I apologize for that. 'Ecumenical' simply means worldwide Christian unity or cooperation. To be ecumenical means to include or incorporate all Christians, whether they are Baptist, Methodist, nondenominational, or any other Christian group."

"Thank you," replied Claude.

"Our liturgy, or our service, is composed of two main parts--the service of the Word and the service of the table. If you don't observe communion, or the Lord's Supper, every week, like we do, then the second part could be called the service of Thanksgiving. The service of the Word includes scripture readings, prayers, songs, the sermon, and a Creed, which is a profession of faith. The service of the table includes the offering, prayers, confession, communion, also called the Lord's Supper, or the Eucharist. The communion includes several prayers mixed with songs before we commune, or receive the body and blood. After we commune, there is a prayer thanking God for feeding us with the spiritual food of bread and wine. Now there is also a beginning and an ending to our service as well. So it could be said that we have a four-part service. The beginning we call entrance rites, or you may recognize it as a call to worship. The ending we call concluding rites, which acts as a dismissal or a sending forth."

There were many questions about the parts of the service, which took much longer than anyone was prepared for. Father Greene suggested some books on liturgical theology that the pastors could read if they were so inclined, but if they were going to get the service planned and rehearsed, they really need to get down to business. He suggested that they break up into groups to work on the service. Half could work on the service of the Word, and the other half could work on the service of the table. Everyone agreed.

Pastor Connelly asked, "Father Greene, I'm guessing our subject or theme would be Thanksgiving, so should we use the Old Testament or the New Testament to pull a scripture reading?"

Father Greene replied, "Why don't we use readings from the Old, the New, a psalm, and a reading from one of the gospels?"

"Four readings?" several asked.

"Sure," said Father Greene. "See if you can find a gospel reading that illuminates the Thanksgiving theme first, then look for readings from the other three that relate to it. It will be a great exercise in creating cohesiveness."

They all looked puzzled, but they accepted the challenge.

As the planning began, Father Greene went around to each group as they worked and answered their questions. Everyone seemed to be enjoying working together, and a bond was starting to form between pastors. They were also finding a deeper meaning in worship planning than merely singing songs and preaching.

Pastor Fred from Corner Street Church asked, "Father Greene, don't we need to contact our worship leaders to get their input on songs?"

Father Greene replied, "Pastor Fred, you are the worship leader."

Pastor Fred said, "No, sir. I'm the pastor. I just preach."

Father Greene said, "As pastor of the church, you are actually the worship leader. You design the service, select the theme, give direction for scripture readings, prayer content, etc. Welcome to your new role."

And they both laughed, as did many others. Some just looked scared.

"Could I have your attention please?" asked Father Greene. "I know that many of you are concerned about the music because you depend on your musicians to make those selections. Your musicians know the repertoire of your congregation. 'Repertoire' simply means the songs that are familiar—that you sing often. In an ecumenical service, we will have to make sure that all the songs we use are familiar to all our congregations if we want them to participate, and we do want them all to participate because worship is not a spectator sport—we all participate."

Several pastors confessed that they have really never paid much attention to the musical selections that were used in their services. They just send a sermon theme to the musicians and let them make the selections. Father Greene suggested that the pastor is actually the worship leader, so that responsibility, or at least oversight, fell on the pastor. Here was a teaching opportunity, and Father Greene loved teaching opportunities.

"May I interrupt your planning, dear friends, to give you some ideas for musical selections?" asked Father Greene.

Many responded with affirmations of "Please do," "Thank you," and even, "God bless you." So Father Greene explained that music should be selected for its function and purpose. "If you need music for a processional—that's when the choir and leaders of the service enter into the sanctuary—then you will want to select a musical piece that you can march to. Typically, that will have a beat in 2 or 4. You wouldn't want to march in to a song that was a waltz—the waltz is typically a 3-beat form and wouldn't be that easy to march to. If you are using music that precedes, supports, or follows a time of prayer, then it should be meditative and not loud or fast. Basically, you would use common sense. The most important part of any song that you select to use would be based on the lyrics. Is it theologically sound? Is it singable? Is it familiar to the people? Is it directed to God from the worshippers? Is it directed to the people from God? Is it directed to each other? All these should be considered when preparing worship for the King of All Creation!"

Again, the pastors were distressed that they had never known these things. At first, they were thinking that maybe Father Greene was making this worship planning too difficult. But as they thought about the King of All Creation, they were convicted that he was right. This service is not for us, but for God.

Another question: "Father Greene, we don't have confession at our church. We believe that confession is a private matter between the individual and God. Furthermore, we don't think that a pastor can forgive sins."

Father Greene said, "You can't go against what you believe. Confession and absolution, or being forgiven, are necessary for a believer before they partake of the body and blood, lest they take it unworthily and bring trouble upon themselves. In fact, 1 Corinthians suggests that you would be sinning against the body and blood of the Lord. Paul could be referring to harboring unconfessed sin while participating in the Lord's Supper. If you don't believe that the pastor has the right to absolve the sins, then the pastor can say, 'Scripture reminds us that when we confess our sins, God is faithful and just to forgive us our sins and cleanse us from all unrighteousness,' and the problem is solved, right?" Again, many looked puzzled, but they agreed.

After some time, they had the first draft of their service together. There was some concern about who would be doing what in the service. Of course, everyone wanted to preach, except Claude, who was strangely very quiet.

Father Greene said, "I'm sure that all of you are quite capable of preaching, but there are just too many of us for that one part. May I suggest that we all consider nominating someone else, not yourself, to fill that role."

They all laughed. As soon as they quieted down, Claude Nelson spoke.

"Father Greene, and all you fine pastors. I agree that you are all well qualified to preach, except for me—I'm not a preacher. I'm here representing our church that is without a preacher for the moment, largely ..."

And there was silence. As tears were streaming down his face, he waited to regain his composure, then continued. "No, entirely due to my interference with God's plan. There is no better Pastor and no better preacher in my opinion than Pastor Marshall."

Everyone knew the story, and all were moved to tears—including Pastor Marshall. Claude found Pastor Marshall, hugged him like a long-lost friend, and they both sobbed.

Father Greene said, "Well, I guess we've found our preacher."

The Final Planning

As the time for the Community Thanksgiving Gathering, as it had been named--drew near, there were meetings being held all over town. Some were planning events like sack races, horseshoes, dunk tanks and the like, while others were planning for food vendors, trinket stores and social needs. There were raffles and drawings and races—everything you could image was being planned. But in Father Greene's mind, the most important thing... and the thing that would be most important to break down barriers and bond people together was the worship service that the whole community would share. This was the opportunity to bring Faithville into a unified, faith-based community.

The pastors of all the churches in the community continued to meet either physically at one location or virtually on their computers. Their planning became exceptionally involved with research, questions, soul searching, changing viewpoints, and more. Pastors from differing faith traditions were having coffee with others to share thoughts, beliefs, and scriptural understanding with other pastors. It was what you would expect from a college or seminary campus where ministry students were searching for spiritual truths. Barriers were being broken, bonds were being created—God was at work, mending broken relationships and tearing down barriers that had separated denominations and kept them from communicating for decades.

The pastors had been connected with an online application where they could collaborate together in their planning. It was in this application that they were able to construct the service in its entirety, and all the other pastors were able to see and comment.

As Father Greene was looking at the service and all the pastors that were participating, he noticed that the pastors that had closed their churches weren't included. As he remembered hearing about the closing of their churches, his heart was crushed. He thought for a few minutes about how devastating that must have been for them to have to close their doors after a history of ministry that they had shared. There were years of sermons, planning events, ministering to the sick and the needy, going through struggles, and watching God work through His people. And then, having to close their doors.

Tears filled his eyes as he felt the pain of his colleagues in ministry. Immediately, he had Mrs. Alexander created a list of the pastors of the closed churches. He preceded to call them and invited them all the meet him at Dauphy's Diner for lunch.

The next day, Father Greene had lunch with the pastors of the six closed churches. As they ate and talked about the history of their churches, it was clear that these were all faithful, God-fearing ministers, called by God to serve Him in truth and righteousness. They had done nothing wrong. They were just victims of the economy and their congregations wanting something they couldn't afford. Their people had been swept away by new paint, new sounds, new sights, and new hopes. In Father Greene's mind, the people had abandoned their family for dreams.

At that point, the Holy Spirit spoke to Father Greene and charged him—yes, convicted him to fix it.

Father Greene wrote a letter to all the pastors of the community and told them about his conviction. He said in the letter that these six church pastors were faithful men of God who had provided for their congregations for many years and that they now had lost the major portion of their members to other churches and had to close. He pleaded with the pastors to please allow them to be included in the planning of the Community Thanksgiving Gathering even though they were no longer active pastors in the community.

To Father Greene's surprise, every pastor responded with a hearty "yes!" The Holy Spirit was moving among the pastors of the community!

The truth was that the decades of division among the people in Faithville was initiated by the pastors—both past and present. They had instilled in their people that their denominational doctrines and beliefs were right and all the others were wrong. In their defense, that was what they were taught by their predecessors and their denominational agencies and conferences. That didn't make it right. It was time for a change.

The six pastors were incorporated into the planning teams, and their input was welcomed. They had some of the same questions as the other pastors, but their questions were all answered by the community pastors, and the planning continued.

Everyone was assigned a part in the service. After they had studied up on the Lord's Supper, they all agreed that they wanted to have a communitywide Lord's Supper. They also decided they wanted it to be sacramental in nature, and not just a memorial or a "remembrance" of the Lord's crucifixion and resurrection, but a genuine real-presence communion. They also agreed that Father Greene should orchestrate that part of the service.

Father Greene was happy to accept the honor. He looked over the service and was amazed that these pastors had come together from all their unrelated theologies to create a service of worship that was theologically sound and ecumenically acceptable. The scripture readings all related to giving thanks to God for all that He has provided for them. They had included songs that were singable, known, and worked well for where they were placed. They had included prayers for the people that included general to specific needs. They had included a confession, and even an absolution. They had incorporated the Nicene Creed, the Lord's Prayer, communion, a thank-you prayer for feeding them with spiritual food, and a benediction to send them out to do God's work.

It was a wonderful service plan. Pastor Marshall had even sent Father Greene a draft of his sermon that combined all the readings into a message that dwelt on thankfulness and unity.

Father Greene was overjoyed with all that had been planned. He stopped and prayed. With great emotion in his heart, he thanked God for all that was happening through His divine interaction with the Holy Spirit. He thanked God for Faithville and the possibility of change that awaited them in the near future. He also prayed for the restoration of the closed churches and the renewal of worship in all the churches in the city.

As he ended his prayer, he confessed to God how unworthy he was to receive such a blessing, but he thanked Him just the same.

The Gathering

The day had finally come. It looked like the entire town turned out. There were people everywhere. The local newspaper had invited everyone, and so had everyone on social media. Families had invited their relatives from neighboring towns. There was an early estimate that more than five thousand people came to the Community Thanksgiving Gathering.

The festivities started at 10:00 a.m. in the town square. There was food, music, rides, races, and competitions of all sorts. There were baking contests and raffles that drew in lots of money. Everyone appeared happy and content. Baptists were running events with Methodists, and Presbyterians were running events with Lutherans. Nondenominational groups were running events with Catholics. It was like heaven came to earth, if even for just a while. The whole town was like a new place!

As the evening drew to an end, the announcement came through the loudspeakers that the gathering was coming to a close and that everyone was invited to the town hall for a closing worship service.

Not everyone stayed, but there were still about three thousand that did stay—mainly the townspeople. They headed for the town hall and began filling the seats.

As the hour approached, Father Greene addressed the people: "Dear friends, please find a seat. I'm not sure you can all be seated, but if you can find a place to stand in the back, that will be fine. We are gathered here tonight to worship together as a unified body of believers. We are divided by denominations and have been for a very long time. All the pastors of our city have planned for an ecumenical service tonight.

"'Ecumenical' simply means all-inclusive. So it doesn't matter what denomination you are—this service is designed for everyone. It was totally designed by all the community pastors for all Christians in the community. We are one body in Christ. Tonight we are not divided by denominational differences. So as we quiet ourselves to worship, please remember that. Tonight, my friends, we are one body of believers—one God, one faith, one baptism."

With that, the service began.

There was a group of musicians assembled in the balcony area that no one could see—the people could only hear the music they produced. It was a wonderful sound created by woodwinds and vocal sounds—no words.

As they were presenting, a pastor walked up to the front, stood before a microphone, and said, "Oh, come, let us worship and bow down. Let us kneel before the Lord, our Maker!"[5]

Some people were so moved by this psalm, they bowed their heads, got down on their knees and began to pray. As the pastor exited, the musicians began to play "Joyful, Joyful, We Adore Thee." The words were displayed on the screens, and everyone began to sing. The sound filled the space with excitement!

As the song ended, another pastor walked up to the lectern, on the left side, and began reading from the Old Testament, first saying, "A reading from the book we love." And he continued, "Deuteronomy 26:1-11 says,"

---

[5]   Psalm 95:6 (English Standard Version).

When you have entered the land the Lord your God is giving you as an inheritance and have taken possession of it and settled in it, take some of the firstfruits of all that you produce from the soil of the land the Lord your God is giving you and put them in a basket. Then go to the place the Lord your God will choose as a dwelling for his Name and say to the priest in office at the time, "I declare today to the Lord your God that I have come to the land the Lord swore to our ancestors to give us." The priest shall take the basket from your hands and set it down in front of the altar of the Lord your God. Then you shall declare before the Lord your God: "My father was a wandering Aramean, and he went down into Egypt with a few people and lived there and became a great nation, powerful and numerous. But the Egyptians mistreated us and made us suffer, subjecting us to harsh labor. Then we cried out to the Lord, the God of our ancestors, and the Lord heard our voice and saw our misery, toil and oppression. So the Lord brought us out of Egypt with a mighty hand and an outstretched arm, with great terror and with signs and wonders. He brought us to this place and gave us this land, a land flowing with milk and honey; and now I bring the firstfruits of the soil that you, Lord, have given me." Place the basket before the Lord your God and bow down before him. Then you and the Levites and the foreigners residing

among you shall rejoice in all the good things the
Lord your God has given to you and your household.[6]

At the conclusion of the reading, he said, "This is the Word of
the Lord."

And the people followed the prompting from the screen and
responded, "Thanks be to God."

As he exited, another pastor approached the lectern and asked
that everyone stand. He said, "Reading from Psalm 100. I will read
to the asterisk if you will complete the verse."

The screen prompted them.

Leader: Shout for joy to the Lord, all the earth. *

People: Worship the Lord with gladness; come before him with
          joyful songs.

Leader: Know that the Lord is God. *

People: It is he who made us, and we are his, we are his people,
          the sheep of his pasture.

Leader: Enter his gates with thanksgiving and his courts with
          praise; *

People: give thanks to him and praise his name.

Leader: For the Lord is good and his love endures forever; *

People: his faithfulness continues through all generations.[7]

Another pastor came to the lectern. He asked everyone to be
seated and then said, "Another reading from the book we love.
Philippians 4:4-9 reads,"

---

[6]   Deuteronomy 26:1–11 (New International Version)
[7]   Psalm 100 (New International Version)

Rejoice in the Lord always; again I will say, Rejoice. Let all men know your forbearance. The Lord is at hand. Have no anxiety about anything, but in everything by prayer and supplication with thanksgiving let your requests be made known to God. And the peace of God, which passes all understanding, will keep your hearts and your minds in Christ Jesus.

Finally, brethren, whatever is true, whatever is honorable, whatever is just, whatever is pure, whatever is lovely, whatever is gracious, if there is any excellence, if there is anything worthy of praise, think about these things. What you have learned and received and heard and seen in me, do; and the God of peace will be with you.[8]

He ended the reading by saying, "The Word of the Lord." Everyone followed the prompts on the screen and said, "Thanks be to God."

The musicians began to play "Alleluia." Everyone was asked to stand for the gospel reading, and they sang together from the words on the screen. As the verse ended, Reverend Jane, who was assigned to read the gospel passage, said, "I read from the gospel of Saint John." And she continued, "John 6:25–35 says,"

When they found him on the other side of the sea, they said to him, "Rabbi, when did you come here?" Jesus answered them, "Truly, truly, I say to you, you seek me, not because you saw signs, but because you

---

[8]   Philippians 4:4–9 (Revised Standard Version)

ate your fill of the loaves. Do not labor for the food which perishes, but for the food which endures to eternal life, which the Son of man will give to you; for on him has God the Father set his seal." Then they said to him, "What must we do, to be doing the works of God?" Jesus answered them, "This is the work of God, that you believe in him whom he has sent." So they said to him, "Then what sign do you do, that we may see, and believe you? What work do you perform? Our fathers ate the manna in the wilderness; as it is written, 'He gave them bread from heaven to eat.'" Jesus then said to them, "Truly, truly, I say to you, it was not Moses who gave you the bread from heaven; my Father gives you the true bread from heaven. For the bread of God is that which comes down from heaven, and gives life to the world." They said to him, "Lord, give us this bread always."

Jesus said to them, "I am the bread of life; he who comes to me shall not hunger, and he who believes in me shall never thirst.[9]

When she finished reading, she said, "This is the gospel of the Lord."

The people replied, following the words on the screen, "Praise to you, Lord Christ!"

Then Pastor Marshall walked up to the pulpit prepared on the other side of the stage area.

---

[9]   John 6:25–35 (Revised Standard Version)

"Dear friends, my name is Rick Marshall, and it's an honor to be able to come and speak to you this evening. I have been a minister pretty much all of my adult life and have preached all over place. I have been a part of Faithville for the past ten years and have grown to love this town and all of you very much.

"I have been asked to do what I consider impossible, but we all know that with God, nothing is impossible, right?"

There were several "Amens."

"I have been asked to speak at this Community Thanksgiving Gathering on the subject of thanksgiving and unity. I did not get to select the passage, or in this case, the passages because all the pastors came together to do the planning. Father Greene explained to us the reasons why we worship and some ideas that make sense. One of those ideas was to use scripture passages from the Old Testament, the Psalms, the New Testament, and the Gospel that all somehow relate to the subject.

"Now, to me, that sounds totally impossible, but after studying what my colleagues have selected, I do see how they all interrelate, and I would like to share that with you now.

"In the Old Testament, we see how God brought His people out of slavery. He did the same for us, in a different way. After they were freed and entered the land that the Lord had promised them, there were instructions as to how they were to live and what they were supposed to do. They were to bring the first fruits of the land to the Lord, bow before Him, and, together with everyone, celebrate with all the bounty that the Lord their God had given them.

"In a way, we do this too, with our tithes and offerings. We also do this with our service and with our sacrifices of time and talents. My question about this is: Do we do it through our love for God, or is it a feeling of duty? Do we freely give, or do we sometimes attach strings? We need to see with different eyes—through the eyes of Jesus.

"How are we to serve our Lord? We are to be joyful in the Lord and serve Him with gladness. When we come before Him, we should have a song in our hearts—singing aloud or just in our hearts as we joyfully serve Him. God made us, and we belong to Him. He is our Shepherd, and we are His sheep. We should thank Him, praise Him, and call on His Name more often than we do. He has shown us mercy, and His faithfulness will always endure.

"We should rejoice in the Lord every day, and even every moment. We should be gentle people, kind people, loving people, and everyone should see it in is. I am reminded of a song, 'They Will Know We Are Christians by Our Love.' We do not have to worry about anything, but we should always pray, being thankful when we make our requests to God. When we do this, we will have peace that cannot be understood. That peace will guard our hearts and minds in Christ Jesus.

"So then, whatever is true, honorable, just, pure, pleasing, commendable, and if there is any excellence, and if there is anything worthy of praise, just ... just stop and think about that. We need to keep doing what we have learned, received, heard, and seen in Jesus. If we do, then God's peace will cover us.

"For years, this town has been torn by division between political parties, skin color, finances, and sadly, by religious and denominational barriers. We look down our noses at other religions because we do not understand them—and fear comes from not knowing. Even in our own religion, Christianity, we look down our noses on other Christians that are not of our denomination. Yes, unfortunately, it is true. I've overhead many of you making comments about other denominations in the grocery store, the restaurants, and the barbershop. You cannot deny it—you must own it. I do not want to sound like John the Baptizer, but, friends, we have to repent! Let us turn from our sinful ways and refocus ourselves on living righteous lives. Don't you want peace? We need to see with different eyes—through the eyes of Jesus.

"The reading from the gospel of John starts just after Jesus had performed the miracle of feeding five thousand people with five loaves of bread and two fish. You can read it for yourselves by starting at the beginning of chapter 6. To paraphrase, Jesus took the loaves, after he had given thanks, and gave them to the people. He did the same with the fish. After everyone had finished eating their fill, He had the disciples gather what was left over so nothing would be wasted. They filled twelve large baskets with leftovers from the five barley loaves. Now that's a miracle that brings tears to my eyes. God loves us and provides for us—He feeds us.

"After that, Jesus slipped away from the crowd to be alone. That night, the disciples got in their boat and headed back to Capernaum. A huge wind blew in and churned the water. They looked and saw Jesus walking on the water, and they were scared out of their minds. Jesus got in the boat and continued to Capernaum with them.

"The people realized that Jesus was gone and was not likely to return, so they piled into a boat and headed out to find Him. Our gospel reading for today begins where they found Him.

"They wanted to know when Jesus got there, but Jesus knew why they came. He said, and I am paraphrasing, 'You didn't come looking for me because you saw God's hand at work, but because I fed you with free food.' Jesus was trying to teach them something especially important when he told them not to work for food that will perish, but for food that endures for eternal life. The food that only Jesus could give them.

"Friends, I must admit that I have read this passage many times and never really picked up on this until now. Jesus wants us to eat Him! What!? You may ask. That is cannibalism! Let us think for a minute. How many times in the scriptures have you heard, 'I am the bread of life'? Unless you eat the flesh of the Son of Man and drink His blood, you do not have life within you. It points straight from the Passover to the cross.

"If you are not familiar with the Passover, go back to the book of Exodus and read it. Briefly, God promised to redeem His people from Egyptian slavery. He sent Moses to Pharaoh with the command to, 'let My people go.' But Pharaoh refused. God sent ten plagues because Pharaoh continued to refuse to let the Israelites go.

"The tenth plague was the worst. It was the death of all the firstborn in Egypt. On that night, God told the Israelites to mark their doorposts and lintels with the blood from a spotless lamb that they would sacrifice. Then, when the Lord passed through the land, He would 'pass over' the houses that had blood on the doorposts and lintels. So it was the 'blood of the spotless Lamb' that saved them. Let me repeat that in a unique way. So it was the 'blood of Jesus' that would save us.

"Do not be confused. Do not be disturbed. I am not changing the words of the scriptures. I am merely sharing with you what I am seeing in the Scriptures. The Passover was to redeem God's people from Egyptian slavery. It was a foreshadowing of what would happen in the future when Jesus's crucifixion, death, and resurrection would redeem us from the slavery of sin. This could only happen through the sacrifice of Jesus as the spotless Lamb.

"So what is Jesus talking about when He alludes to eating His flesh and drinking His blood? It refers to the Lord's Supper that many of us have neglected to partake of regularly. I know that some of our churches only have this observance once or twice a year. Some of our churches celebrate this weekly. The scriptures tell us, 'As often as you do this,' but doesn't dictate how often. I tell you the truth: I think it should be as often as possible.

"Jesus wants us to have peace and to be at peace. This is something that we really can't do on our own. We must repent, which means turn away from lies and deception, or refocus on what is true, honorable, just, pure, pleasing—you know the list. We must have a change of heart. We must learn to be compassionate. Also, we can never grow in our faith if we are not open-minded. We need to see with different eyes—through the eyes of Jesus.

"We are here among people who believe differently than we do. We should learn to acknowledge those differences and understand that there are a variety of interpretations of the words in our Bibles. We are not to judge or pass judgment. We are all brothers and sisters in Christ. We can never be a loving family until we can love those who may believe differently from us.

"In a few minutes, we are going to celebrate Eucharist. Yes, I said it! It's a big word that I recently learned. It means 'great thanksgiving' and we know it as the Lord's Supper, or communion. As we do partake together, would you try to take it differently than you have before. Tonight, would you try to remember the words of Jesus that we just talked about. Would you try to see the bread as Jesus's body, broken for you and for me? And would you try to see the wine as Jesus's blood, spilled out for you and for me?

"I want to share with you one more scripture passage and a story. The passage is from the gospel of John, chapter 17:21-23. It says, 'I pray that they will all be one, just as you and I are one—as you are in me, Father, and I am in you. And may they be in us so that the world will believe you sent me. I have given them the glory you gave me, so they may be one as we are one. I am in them and you are in me. May they experience such perfect unity that the world will know that you sent me and that you love them as much as you love me.'

"When I was in school, our college had a Missions Week, where missionaries from all over the world were invited to come and share with us. There was a missionary to Brazil, named Pastor Mike, who shared with us his journey to Brazil and also planned a worship service so we could experience what their worship was like. Our school was basically all of the same denomination, and we never strayed far from 'our' faith tradition. So this was all quite interesting.

"There were many visitors from different denominations from around the town, and several even came from out of town to hear Pastor Mike speak. My friend Woody was joking and trying to figure out which denomination some of the people were from. I will not share with you his jokes, even though they were funny. They really weren't nice.

"As we continued through the service, there was a time of communion. As the time came, we did not receive the elements at our seats as we were accustomed. Instead, we did it the way they were doing it in Brazil—we came forward in a single file and received the bread and the wine one at a time as we knelt at the rail. First the bread. Then we took a sip of wine.

"After the service, I looked around and found Woody sitting in the back pew. I went over to join him, and as I approached, I noticed that he had been crying. I asked him what was going on, and he said, 'When I took a sip of the wine, I felt it going through my veins. It warmed me. Jesus's blood was traveling through my veins, and His flesh was in my stomach. Jesus is literally in me! And I looked around at the people to my left and my right, that I do not even know, and realized these people that I was joking about are my brothers and sisters in Christ. Jesus is in them as well.' At that point, Woody just began sobbing uncontrollably.

"Jesus spoke to my friend Woody through communion, and it changed his life forever. Woody became a pastor and is currently serving in another state, in a different denomination. I am not saying that something spectacular is going to happen to you tonight during communion, but I am saying that if you will open your heart and your mind, Jesus is ready to jump in and make a change—in the Name of the Father, and of the Son, and of the Holy Spirit. Amen."

Pastor Marshall made his way back to his seat as another pastor made his way to the front and asked everyone to stand. He said, "Let us affirm our faith by reciting the Nicene Creed."

The words appeared on the screen, and they began.

We believe in one God,
    the Father, the Almighty,
    maker of heaven and earth,
    of all that is, seen and unseen.

We believe in one Lord, Jesus Christ,
    the only Son of God,
    eternally begotten of the Father,
    God from God, Light from Light,
    true God from true God,
    begotten, not made,
    of one Being with the Father.
    Through him all things were made.
    For us and for our salvation
        he came down from heaven:
    by the power of the Holy Spirit

he became incarnate from the Virgin Mary,
and was made man.
For our sake he was crucified under Pontius Pilate;
he suffered death and was buried.
On the third day he rose again
in accordance with the Scriptures;
he ascended into heaven
and is seated at the right hand of
the Father.
He will come again in glory to judge the living and
the dead,
and his kingdom will have no end.

We believe in the Holy Spirit, the Lord, the giver
of life, who proceeds from the Father and the Son.
With the Father and the Son he is worshiped
and glorified.
He has spoken through the Prophets.
We believe in one holy catholic and
apostolic Church.
We acknowledge one baptism for the forgiveness
of sins.
We look for the resurrection of the dead,
and the life of the world to come. Amen.[10]

Another pastor went up to the lectern and asked everyone to remain standing for the Prayers. He asked that at the end of each prayer, as prompted on the screen, to respond with, "Lord, please hear our prayer." They prayed for general things, like the world, the

---

[10] Https://www.bcponline.org, *The Online Book of Common Prayer*, 358–359.

nation, and the economy. They prayed for less general things like their towns, their jobs, and their sick. Finally, they prayed for more specific things like their faith, their frailty, and the sin in their lives.

As the pastor was leaving the stage, yet another came and asked that everyone remain standing. He said, "We all have sin in our lives—known sins and unknown sins. We are about to celebrate communion, and we should not enter into communion with our Lord if we have something against our brother or our sister. Please, if you have issues with your neighbor, go, right now, and make it right with them. Forgive one another and make it right, or forgo taking communion until you do."

There was movement in the town hall, so he paused. There was a lot of movement. People were actually going over to their neighbors and confessing to one another the issues they had. There was murmuring. There was weeping. There was embracing. Hearts were being healed, and lives were being changed. The Holy Spirit was convicting, and people were responding. It was a glorious time!

After what must have been fifteen minutes, the pastor continued. "Let us humbly confess our sins to Almighty God."

And they began.

Most merciful God,
we confess that we have sinned against you
in thought, word, and deed,
by what we have done,
and by what we have left undone.
We have not loved you with our whole heart;
we have not loved our neighbors as ourselves.
We are truly sorry and we humbly repent.
For the sake of your Son Jesus Christ,

have mercy on us and forgive us;

that we may delight in your will,

and walk in your ways,

to the glory of your Name. Amen.[11]

The pastor leading the confession was the same pastor who had earlier said, "Father Greene, we don't have confession at our church. We believe that confession is a private matter between the individual and God."

His name was Pastor Luke Matthews. He now understood the power of confession—how it could move people to unashamedly reconcile their differences with their neighbors in front of God and man. He was so moved he could hardly speak. But he did. He held his hand out over the crowd of people and led them in prayer:

> Almighty God have mercy on you, forgive you all your sins through our Lord Jesus Christ, strengthen you in all goodness, and by the power of the Holy Spirit keep you in eternal life. Amen.[12]

Pastor Matthews addressed the people. "I have learned something new that I would like to share with you. A term called 'passing the peace,' and we are going to do it in just a moment. Several of our churches have a time, usually at the beginning of our services, where we welcome one another. I must admit that I like that time. I like it a lot! But it's really not a holy time. People aren't in a spiritual mood. They say, 'Hey buddy, how are you doing? How's the family?' and stuff like that. Tonight we are going to make it a holy time. We are going to turn to those around us and say, 'The peace of the Lord be

---

[11] Https://www.bcponline.org (The Online Book of Common Prayer), 360.

[12] Ibid.

with you.' And we are to respond with something holy. We are going to respond with, 'And also with you.' If I've learned anything over the past few weeks of joining with my fellow pastors to plan this service, it's that the time we spend together worshiping God needs to be a holy time. So let's keep it holy and give this a try."

And with that, he held out his hands toward the people as if he was holding something and said, "The peace of the Lord be always with you."

And the people responded, "And also with you."

Then he said, "Please pass the peace to your neighbors."

People were trying this "new thing" with their neighbors. At first they thought it frivolous, but the more they did it, the more they found holiness in the words. It seemed to be a more valuable way to greet someone than, "Hey, how have you been?" Many of them actually preferred it.

Another pastor went up to the front and told the people that this was not an intermission, but in this type of service, there is a change, of sorts, from the first part called the service of the Word to the second part called the service of the table. As everyone found their seat and the musicians began to play a meditative tune, the ushers began to carry buckets around the crowd to collect offerings. People had been so moved throughout the service so far that they had the users wait while they dug through their purses and wallets to find an offering. The musicians were not prepared for such a long offering and had to repeat their musical selection three times before the ushers had collected all the gifts.

The offerings were then processed to the front, where Father Greene was waiting. He received them, held them up to the Lord, and said,

Yours, O Lord, is the greatness, and the power, and the glory, and the victory, and the majesty: for everything in heaven and on earth is yours; yours is the Kingdom, O Lord, and you are exalted as Head above all. All things come from you, O Lord.[13]

And the people responded, following the words on the screen, "And of your own have we given you."[14]

Father Greene made the sign of the cross over the offering and handed it to one of the ushers to put away.

Father Greene knew that the majority of the people had never been to a Eucharistic service, and he wasn't sure how it would be received. He thought it might be a good idea to narrate the service as they progressed through it.

He said, "Dear people, it is not our desire to confuse you. I know that many of you have not attended liturgical services in the past. If you were raised in a liturgical tradition, you have an idea of what's going on, but if you haven't, you could be completely lost and confused. Therefore, I think it might be a good idea that I narrate what's going on so that you might understand more completely."

He cleared his throat and continued, "The screen has been prepared with slides that will guide you. Your part is boldfaced, so just follow along. I will attempt to give you guidance as we move through the service of the table."

He continued, "The first part is called the Sursum Corda. I assure you that all these things are derived from the Bible. David uses this expression in the Psalms to describe his desire to worship

---

[13] Anglican Church in North America, *The Book of Common Prayer and Administration of the Sacraments* (Anglican Liturgy Press, 2019), p. 131.

[14] Ibid.

the Lord and commune with Him. Jeremiah uses the same phrase in Lamentations, so here we go."

> Leader: The Lord be with you.
>
> People: And also with you.
>
> Leader: Lift up your hearts.
>
> People: We lift them up to the Lord.
>
> Leader: Let us give thanks to the Lord our God.
>
> People: It is right to give Him thanks and praise.

> It is right, our duty and our joy, always and everywhere to give thanks to you, Father Almighty, Creator of heaven and earth.[15]

Father Greene said, "So far so good. Now, there is a prayer called the Proper Preface, and it is selected according to the season of occasion. I have selected this one."

> Because the wonders of your Creation reflect your goodness and beauty; and your gifts of sun and rain, seed-time and harvest, manifest your constant love and care for all that you have made.[16]

> Therefore we praise you, joining our voices with Angels and Archangels and with all the company of heaven, who for ever sing this hymn to proclaim the glory of your Name:[17]

---

[15] Https://www.bcponline.org. *The Online Book of Common Prayer*, 361.

[16] Anglican Church in North America, *Book of Common Prayer* (2019), 156.

[17] Ibid., 132.

Father Greene stopped and said, "This is called the Sanctus, which means, 'Holy, Holy, Holy Lord.'" The musicians started the introduction to "Holy, Holy, Holy," which everyone knew. The words were on the screen, so everyone sang together. As they finished the song, Father Greene said, "Next is a prayer of consecration. It is a time where we remember the betrayal and suffering of our Lord. It is also a time where we remember and relive the Last Supper that our Lord had with His disciples. It is in these prayers that the elements become for us His body and His blood."

Holy and gracious Father: In your infinite love you made us for yourself; and when we had sinned against you and become subject to evil and death, you, in your mercy, sent your only Son Jesus Christ into the world for our salvation. By the Holy Spirit and the Virgin Mary he became flesh and dwelt among us. In obedience to your will, he stretched out his arms upon the Cross and offered himself once for all, that by his suffering and death we might be saved. By his resurrection he broke the bonds of death, trampling Hell and Satan under his feet. As our great high priest, he ascended to your right hand in glory, that we might come with confidence before the throne of grace.

On the night that he was betrayed, our Lord Jesus Christ took bread; and when he had given thanks, he broke it, and gave it to his disciples, saying, 'Take, eat; this is my Body, which is given for you: Do this in remembrance of me.'[18]

Father Greene had lifted the bread for all to see and then returned it to the table.

> Likewise, after supper, Jesus took the cup, and when he had given thanks, he gave it to them, saying, 'Drink from this, all of you; for this is my Blood of the New Covenant, which is shed for you, and for many, for the forgiveness of sins: Whenever you drink it, do this in remembrance of me.'[19]

Father Greene had lifted the cup for all to see, then returned it to the table.

Then he said, "This is called the memorial acclamation." Following the prompts on the screen, the people said together, "Christ has died, Christ is risen, Christ will come again."[20] Then Father Greene continued with his prayers.

> We celebrate the memorial of our redemption, O Father, in this sacrifice of praise and thanksgiving, and we offer you these gifts. Sanctify them by your Word and the Holy Spirit to be for your people the Body and Blood of your Son Jesus Christ.[21]

---

[18] Ibid., 132–133.
[19] Ibid., 133.
[20] Ibid.
[21] Ibid., 133–134.

At this point, Father Greene made a sign of the cross over the elements of bread and wine.

> Sanctify us also, that we may worthily receive this holy Sacrament, and be made one body with him, that he may dwell in us and we in him. In the fullness of time, put all things in subjection under your Christ, and bring us with all your saints into the joy of our heavenly kingdom where we shall see our Lord face to face. All this we ask through your Son Jesus Christ: By him, and with him, and in him, in the unity of the Holy Spirit, all honor and glory is yours, Almighty Father, now and for ever. Amen.[22]

Father Greene said, "And now, as our Savior Christ has taught us, we are bold to pray."

And everyone joined:

Our Father, Who art in heaven,
  hallowed be thy Name,
  thy kingdom come,
  thy will be done,
  on earth as it is in heaven.
Give us this day our daily bread.
And forgive us our trespasses,
  as we forgive those
  who trespass against us.
And lead us not into temptation,
  but deliver us from evil.

---

[22] Ibid., 134.

For thine is the kingdom,
>   and the power, and the glory,
>   for ever and ever. Amen.[23]

Father Greene said, "Christ our Passover Lamb has been sacrificed, once for all upon the Cross." And the people following the prompts on the screen, responded, "Therefore let us keep the feast."[24]

Father Greene told the people that the next song is called Agnus Dei, which means, 'Lamb of God,' you take away the sins of the world. They sang together following the words on the screen.

As they sang, ushers invited the people to walk down the aisles to the front to receive the Body and the Blood of Christ. This was new for them. They had always received the elements while sitting in their seats. They were given instructions to hold one hand over the other to receive the Body. After receiving the Body and e5698ating it, they were to receive the Blood. To receive it, they were to take a sip. Many were skeptical about taking a sip of alcohol in a religious setting such as this, but they did it anyway and then returned to their seats.

After hearing the sermon about unity, thanksgiving, and even Pastor Marshall's story about his friend Woody, the people went back to their seats and either meditated or got on their knees and prayed. Things were happening that could not be explained.

As the service came to a close, Father Greene spoke to the people. "My friends, it has been an honor to worship with you tonight. It is my hope that this service has not been completely foreign to you. All the pastors from Faithville have joined together to plan this service and have agreed on everything we have done tonight. Together we have planned, and together we have bonded. Judging

---

23   Ibid.
24   Ibid., 135.

from what I have witnessed tonight, you have also bonded across denominations. Praise be to our God for working in our lives to resurrect relationships. It is my prayer that our Lord will continue to move in our community to restore relationships that have been broken. Our God is able to do all things. Our God is capable to do miracles. Please, my friends, as you leave this place, remember what God has spoken to you."

Another pastor came to the front. He alone was charged with the dismissal. He held his hand out over the crowd and said, "People of God, as you depart from his place, remember that God loves you. Remember that God is not angry with you. Remember that God sacrificed His Son for you because He believes in you. Go out from this place and share the Good News of Christ with the world."

And everyone said, "Amen!"

Chapter

ELEVEN

THE AFTERMATH

The days following the Community Thanksgiving Gathering were amazing! People seemed more relaxed, cheerful, and at peace with themselves and their neighbors. The critical nature of others that had existed for years seemed to have just disappeared overnight. Parties and other social gatherings that had previously been almost exclusively denominational were now accepting of all denominations. There was something very new and very good happening in Faithville.

The pastors of the community had been communicating with each other through email and lunch meetings. They were so excited about what had happened at the service that they wanted to do it again for other occasions. In fact, they had decided to create a group where pastors from all denominations could meet together to fellowship and plan cooperatively within the community. They wanted to call it a Pastors' Association, where they could meet regularly to discuss how they could keep all the denominations working together to glorify God, learn about the other denominational beliefs, and grow in their faith. They had suggested that Father Greene lead this group because of his reputation among the people, as well as among the other pastors. Father Greene was more than happy to accept their offer.

At their very first meeting, one pastor suggested the idea that every month they do a pastoral rotation. As they kicked the idea around, they came up with a motion that every two months, every pastor from another denomination would speak in the church of a different denomination.

For example: The pastor from a Baptist Church would speak in a Presbyterian church, and the pastor from that Presbyterian church would speak in a Methodist church, and that pastor from the Methodist church would speak in a nondenominational church, and so forth. Everyone was in agreement, and a schedule was created. Of course, they would need to get approval from their churches to move forward, but they expected little opposition.

There was also some interest in the areas of the church calendar. Father Greene had shared with the Pastors' Association some of the items that he had covered in workshops he held with his church. The pastors were particularly interested in the church calendar. After an explanation of how the church calendar worked, the majority were in favor of doing a communitywide service of Advent and Lent. Advent was the observance of the weeks preceding the birth of Christ, and Lent was the weeks preceding Easter. It was agreed that the pastors would join together to plan an observance of the events in all their churches. They would study and plan services for their own churches for the season of Advent, and then celebrate together a communitywide Christmas service.

Following that, they would study and plan services for their own churches in observance of Lent, then celebrate together a communitywide Easter service. They thought an Easter sunrise service would be perfect! They could still meet and celebrate their own Easter Service at their own church time if they so desired. It was a wonderful experience!

There were other gatherings that were happening too! Youth groups that were having events, like Youth Lock-Ins, were inviting other youth groups from community churches to join them. No longer were there Baptist Youth Lock-Ins or Methodist Youth Lock-Ins, but now there were just Youth Lock-Ins, and all youth were invited—even if the youth weren't involved with any church! And why not? They were friends who went to the same schools.

There was a group of mission-minded people that decided to create a Missions Ministry in the community that included all denominations. Not only all denominations, but also, all religions. There were some Buddhists, Hindus, and Jews in the community. They were all invited. This organization would provide services, food, and other kinds of help for anyone in need in their community. All the churches of the community met with their congregations and voted to create a line item in their budgets to give a monthly contribution to this organization to help those in need.

Once they were up and running, there were even atheists who were in need that the Missions Ministry was able to help. It wasn't surprising to see some of these atheists show up on a Sunday morning to worship because they had been helped in their hour of need by Christians. Some even became believers in the gospel because of the love shown to them by followers of Jesus.

Several churches had changed the way they thought about worship. They began to think of worship as a whole, instead of music and sermon separately. Some added scripture readings when they previously had none. Some added choruses or psalm readings before prayers. Some even started having frequent communion services because it had such an impact on the people. Prior to the community service, approximately 35 percent of the people in Faithville attended worship on any given Sunday, but now roughly 47 percent of the town was attending.

Things were looking good in Faithville. The effect of many years of dissension between denominations was gone. People were loving each other because they had recognized that they were all brothers and sisters in Christ. Neighbors were helping neighbors—no matter their denominational preference, and more astonishing than that, Christians and other religions were helping each other. The love of God was evident in Faithville.

Father Greene sat in his office looking over his journal entries for the past few months (he made journal entries every day). He noticed a distinct shift in his life and in the life of the community. God had been at work in Faithville since the appearance of the list roughly one year earlier. He thought about all that had transpired. Was it fate, or was it the hand of God?

In Father Green's mind, there was no question. God had intervened. But it wasn't over yet. There were still six churches that had closed. There were still six pastors that were no longer shepherding their flocks. There were still some things that needed to be restored. He asked Mrs. Alexander to contact Reverend Jane and Pastor Marshall to see if they could meet at Dauphy's Diner on Thursday at noon for lunch.

The Three Again

By noon on Thursday, Pastor Marshall, Reverend Jane, and Father Greene met at Dauphy's Diner. Father Greene asked, "Are you all okay in your churches?"

Reverend Jane said, "Yes, I am."

Pastor Marshall said, "I'm not."

Father Greene said, "I am burdened for you, my friend, as well as six other pastors who have no church to serve. This just isn't right, so something must be done. We are the ones who have to fix it."

Reverend Jane and Pastor Marshall just looked perplexed. Pastor Marshall said, "I have no ideas."

Reverend Jane asked, "What can we do?"

Father Greene said, "We can pray, and we can think."

Pastor Marshall asked, "Would it be possible to have them fill in to preach when other pastors are out?"

"That's a great idea," said Reverend Jane.

Father Greene said, "The Pastors' Association is creating a plan to rotate pastors to preach in other churches. I don't see why they should not be included in some capacity."

Pastor Marshall said, "Like me, they don't have a church for another pastor to preach."

Reverend Jane said, "Maybe there will be times during the rotation where some pastors will be out of town, or maybe they could just take the week to visit another church."

"Excellent idea!" said Father Greene. I will discuss this with the other pastors. I'm sure they would be delighted to add them—and you too, Pastor Marshall." Pastor Marshall smiled.

Reverend Jane said, "I could have them on my radio show to share with the people about their journey through this time in their lives. Pastor Marshall, I was already thinking that I would love to have you share next week."

Pastor Marshall was elated! "Seriously? You want me on your radio show?"

"Yes I do," said Reverend Jane. "Just tell me what you want to talk about, and we will make it work."

Father Greene had been thinking while the other two were talking. He said, "Do you think it is possible to find positions in our churches for these pastors during this transitional time for ministry? They are all trained in more than just preaching. It would be a great opportunity for them, and it would be a great help to us."

Pastor Marshall spoke up. "I can't speak for the other pastors, but I would love the opportunity to work with other pastors to see how they do things in their churches. I can help with cleaning, teaching, painting, clerical work—I've been in small churches where the pastor does everything."

Everyone laughed, because they had all been there too.

What would become of the church buildings? Father Greene's heart was broken to think that those precious church buildings would be sold and either destroyed or turned into stores, shops, or bars. He said, "Let's all pray about the church buildings. God must have a plan, and we must figure it out."

They all agreed to pray and think about all they had discussed. Father Greene went back to his office to make notes for the upcoming pastors' meeting. Reverend Jane called her radio show crew and told them to make a spot for Pastor Marshall on the next show. She told them, "We will call it 'A Word from Pastor Marshall,' and he can talk about whatever he wants to."

Pastor Marshall went home and thought about the radio show and what he might talk about.

The Pastors' Meeting

The pastors all met on Thursday evening at the town hall. The mayor had been insistent that the Pastors' Association meet at the town hall as a sign of community support for the churches. Father Greene called the meeting to order. The past meeting notes were reviewed, and a motion was made to accept, seconded and voted into minutes. Questions were asked and answered; then the question for new business was raised. There were suggestions made for new ideas, which were quickly put into the minutes, but were tabled because of so much work that was already on their plates.

Father Greene said, "I am elated that there continues to be new ideas, thoughts, and concerns about what we can and should be doing, but we also need to realize what is currently on our plates. We are planning for Advent, followed by a community Christmas service. Afterward, we move to the planning of Lent and a community Easter sunrise service. And many other things that have already been scheduled. It thrills my heart that we are so full of energy and excitement! Let's make sure we do everything we can, but let's not burn ourselves out in the process.

Pastor George Evans stood and said, "Father Greene, thank you for that comment. Our church is having a massive amount of sickness and deaths because we have an older congregation. I'm working myself silly just trying to keep up. I love what we are doing together as an association of pastors, but I feel guilty about the time I'm spending with my own people and not having the stamina necessary to keep up with everything."

"Pastor George," said Father Greene, "we do understand, and we all have our responsibilities to our own congregations first."

Several other pastors agreed, and few said, "Amen."

Father Greene said, "I have an idea that I wanted to share with you all that might help lighten our burdens. There are seven pastors in our city that are now without churches. They are all fine men that have led churches for years and have experience in all areas of ministry. Would it be helpful if we incorporated these men into our churches for a season to help us?"

They thought for a few minutes and talked among themselves. Finally, one pastor spoke up and said, "Father Greene, that's a wonderful idea!"

Another pastors said, "What if we don't have funds to pay them?"

Father Greene said, "I have no idea, but my assumption is that these men would see the opportunity to serve God as a privilege. I'm sure they would appreciate anything you could give, but we can only ask."

The seven pastors that Father Greene mentioned were present at the meeting because they had been invited. One of them stood up and said, "I'm one of the pastors that is currently without a congregation. My name is Bobby Franks. Our church had to close because we couldn't afford to pay our bills. I can only speak for me, but I would love to serve the Lord in any capacity. I don't have to be paid. I found a part-time job at the funeral home. So please, let me help you."

Pastor George stood up and said, "Brother Bobby, would you come help us?"

Pastor Bobby said, "It would be an honor, Pastor George. I'll be at your church first thing in the morning."

The other six pastors, including Pastor Marshall, stood up to offer their help. Father Greene asked Pastor Marshall to please be seated.

Pastor Marshall said, "But, Father Greene, I'm available to help too."

Father Greene said, "No. You have already been suggested by our church leadership to help at Holy Cross, if you will accept."

Pastor Marshall's emotions overtook him so that he couldn't speak. He just nodded and sat down. Within just a few short minutes, all the pastors had a new church to serve. Though it might only be for a season, they had a church home.

"There is one more item I wish to bring before you all tonight," said Father Greene. "It's not something that can be dealt with tonight, but it's something that we can pray about and think on. I believe that prayer can bring things about, if it's God's will. I also believe that God gave us brains to think with and aid us in discovering His will. So ponder this: There are six churches in our community that have had to close. This absolutely breaks my heart. These churches were built by congregations that love God with all their hearts. They put their money, their time, and their talents into these buildings. Now they are abandoned. Someone or some company will purchase them from the lending companies and turn them into stores, shops, nightclubs, or anything else. Steeples that once signified a house of worship will be removed. Pews will be used for scrap wood and any stained glass which tells the gospel story will be replaced with glass or something else. My question to you is this, is there anything we can do to keep these churches from being sold?"

There was only silence, and the silence was deafening. While it was only a few minutes, it felt like hours.

Finally someone spoke. "The word on the street is that there will be an auction, and the highest bidder over what is owed to the bank will be the new owner."

"My brothers," said Father Greene, "we have to pray for divine intervention. In my faith tradition, everything that is set aside for the Lord's work is consecrated for that purpose. Those items, be it a person, chalice, or a musical instrument, if it's consecrated, it should be considered forever holy. Please start praying for wisdom in what we should do, but also think. Ask your friends and acquaintances what can be done, if anything."

Then they broke up into smaller groups and continued planning for the season of Advent that was soon to arrive.

Chapter

TWELVE

THE RESOLVE

Pastor Marshall was troubled about how everything had transpired over the past year. Three churches were introduced to a list that would promote church growth. Jump ahead about a year, and three churches had grown at the expense of six churches that had to close because of loss of members—and thus finances—to the three churches that were growing. Though it was spread out over a year, it just seemed suspicious that the three churches were targeted. As he pondered why there were three churches targeted, he wondered if there was a mischievous motive behind it all.

He researched all the public records and found that T&A Finance was the holder for all the loans for the new church growth list. They were the only company that would secure a loan for Holy Cross, Freedom Church, and New Life Church. Were they victims of a scam?

He did further research and found that the president of T&A Finance was none other than Ted Wilson. Oh wow! The very one that presented the initial list. T&A Finance was controlled by Ted and Alicia Wilson!

He immediately went to Father Greene's office. Mrs. Alexander said that Father Greene was in a meeting, so Pastor Marshall paced the hall waiting until he was free. As he paced, he kept running everything through his mind. Why would they do this? Was he misreading the information? Could he be wrong? He was so confused!

Finally, Mrs. Alexander said, "Father Greene is free now."

He rushed into Father Greene's office and just started gabbling about everything he had learned.

Father Greene said, "Pastor Marshall, please calm down and take a seat."

Pastor Marshall said, "Father Greene, I may be wrong, but it seems we have all been scammed!"

Father Greene said, "I've suspected that from when we tried to get a loan. T&A Finance was a bit too obvious, but I haven't been sure. Please tell me what you have discovered."

Pastor Marshall explained what he had researched, and Father Greene agreed that they had been scammed. It all made sense. "What can we do?" asked Pastor Marshall.

Father Greene said, "There's only one thing we can do. We must find them and confront them."

They took off to the police station to visit with Chief Peters.

The chief greeted them with the usual niceties and asked them to come into his office. "What can I help you gentlemen with?" asked the chief.

Pastor Marshall started with, "We've been scammed!"

Father Greene stopped him and asked, "Chief Peters, I wonder if you have an address for Ted and Alicia Wilson. We would like to visit with them."

Chief Peters said, "Actually, I do. When I was checking them out earlier, I found that they are living at the farm they acquired from Jake Miller."

Father Greene said, "Thank you so much."

Chief Peters asked if there was a problem.

Father Greene said, "No problem. We just wanted to visit with them."

Father Greene and Pastor Marshall headed to Jake Miller's farm. Pastor Marshall was concerned. "What are we going to do? What are we going to ask them?"

Father Greene said, "We are just going to visit them to see how they are doing."

Pastor Marshall wasn't convinced. He thought there was going to be a confrontation.

When they arrived, they found both Ted and Alicia around back in the garden. They were planting vegetables.

Father Greene said, "How are you doing?"

Ted said, "Father Greene, thanks for coming by. We are doing well. What brings you out?"

"Well," Father Greene said, "we haven't visited with you in quite a while. We just wanted to see how you are doing and to visit with you a while."

Alicia said, "Shall we go inside and have some tea?"

Father Greene said, "That would be very nice."

After some talk about the weather, the economy, and such, Ted said, "Father Greene and Pastor Marshall, we have something to tell you."

Father Greene asked if it was a confession. If so, he would need to retrieve his stole from the car.

Ted said, "No. It's not really a confession but a revelation."

Father Greene said, "Do tell."

It took a while for Ted and Alicia to go through all the details of what took place over the past few years in their lives, and especially the last year. It all came down to the community service.

Ted said, "Father Greene and Pastor Marshall, we are not good people. We came to Faithville with a plan to buy the town."

Pastor Marshall asked, "Whatever do you mean?"

Ted said, "We were going to get your three largest churches to buy into the idea of church growth to pull members from smaller churches to your churches so the smaller churches would close. That way, we could purchase the smaller churches from the lenders for a relatively small price. The larger your churches grew, the more that smaller churches would lose members and have to sell. We would then own all the churches except the three. But our interest rates would balloon to where you couldn't pay, and eventually, you would also have to close. At that point, we would own approximately 50 percent of the property in Faithville."

Father Greene was astonished! "Ted, you speak in past tense. You said you 'were going to,' as if you are no long doing this."

Ted looked at Alicia and smiled. He said, "Yes, past tense. We were going to, but now we're not."

Father Greene said, "I'm confused. What changed your mind? If I might ask."

Alicia spoke first. "It was your community service."

Pastor Marshall asked, "Did our community service change your mind?"

Ted said, "Your community service changed our lives!"

At that point, Alicia started crying.

Pastor Marshall said, "I'm so sorry, did I say something to upset you?" Alicia laughed. "Not at all. We were so moved by the service that we gave our lives to Christ that night. We were both raised with Christian morals. We were in church every week, but we wanted money. We wanted lots of money because we were both raised in poor homes. We found that through lending, we could finagle loan amounts and cause foreclosures. Then we could own property and sell it for a major profit. That's what we had planned for Faithville."

Pastor Marshall asked, "What changed?"

Ted said, "Christ spoke to us during that community service. He didn't speak to just me or just Alicia. He spoke to both of us independently. When we got home that night, we confessed to each other that we had strayed from God and we had been so greedy and self-centered that we had taken advantage of people and wronged them. We decided we had to make it right. We caused six churches to close. The conviction was more than we could stand. So we started praying that God would forgive us. We know in our hearts that God is a loving God and forgives those who truly repent and turn.

"Father Greene and Pastor Marshall, we have turned. But we also have to make it right. We are giving Jake Miller this farm back this week. We will be moving back to our home, but we need to make things right in Faithville as well."

"How will you do that?" asked Fr. Greene.

They just smiled and said, "You will find that out this week."

Then Ted and Alicia got on their knees and said to Father Greene, "Bless us Father, for we have sinned."

The auction for the six church properties was canceled. There was a write-up in the local paper that the auction was canceled because the lender had forgiven all the debts, as theirs had been forgiven.

There were six churches that were now the property of the Pastors' Association, as the deed signed by the lender had stated. One was used as a recreation center for boys needing a safe place to play. One was used as a soup kitchen for folks who had lost their way in life. One was used for a community outreach center, where people could go to receive education and training for trades. One was used for a radio station.

Reverend Jane was elated to have a local radio station. One was used for a prayer garden, where townspeople could go to reflect and meditate on the goodness of God. One was used as an interfaith chapel. People of all religions and faiths could go there to worship, pray, learn, and fellowship together.

Father Greene was insistent that the sanctuary of each of the six churches be used only for what it was consecrated to be—a house of worship.

The End

www.ingramcontent.com/pod-product-compliance
Lightning Source LLC
Chambersburg PA
CBHW021016180626
46814CB00003B/1310